IT WAS THE MOST RIDICULOUS THING in the entire world: Kyra, would-be assassin and master potioner, had resorted to hunting down her prey—her best friend the princess—with a piglet.

But she had no choice. The princess had to die.

Didn't she?

A twist of doubt swirled through Kyra. What if she was wrong?

POISON

BRIDGET ZINN

HYPERION
NEW YORK

Copyright © 2013 by Bridget Zinn

All rights reserved. Published by Hyperion, an imprint of Disney Book Group.
No part of this book may be reproduced or transmitted in any form
or by any means, electronic or mechanical, including photocopying, recording,
or by any information storage and retrieval system, without written permission
from the publisher. For information address Hyperion,
125 West End Avenue, New York, New York 10023.

SUSTAINABLE
FORESTRY
INITIATIVE

Certified Chain of Custody
Promoting Sustainable Forestry
www.sfiprogram.org
SFI-01054
The SFI label applies to the text stock

Printed in the United States of America
First Hyperion paperback edition, 2014
10 9 8 7 6 5 4 3 2 1

V475-2873-0-13349

Library of Congress Control Number for Hardcover: 2012008693
ISBN 978-1-4231-5330-6
Visit www.un-requiredreading.com

for Barrett

One

THE MASTER TRIO POTIONERS' flat didn't *look* impregnable. From the outside it just looked like an enormous ramshackle old house. One in bad need of a paint job.

But Kyra knew better.

The first-floor doors and windows bore elaborate magic wards that would alert the Potioners as soon as Kyra touched a windowsill or doorknob. And—unless the Potioners had disabled the bellows contraptions Kyra herself had set up— the wards would knock her out with a puff of sleep potion. Only charmed residents could pass when the wards were in place.

No, there was no getting in on the ground floor.

But Kyra also knew there was a window on the second story that had been stuck for years. *That* would be her way in.

Which is why she found herself scaling the side of the old house in broad daylight to clamber in through a half-open window. It wasn't the best idea in the world, but it was Kyra's only option.

Kyra had been watching the house for days.

Once upon a time the home belonged to a wealthy merchant, but there'd been a tragic fire years before that had killed Lloyd Newman and his family. These days it was split into four apartments. The downstairs was occupied by two noisy families, and in one of the upstairs units lived an old hermit named Ellie.

Then there was the fourth apartment.

The illustrious Master Trio Potioners' lodgings. The one she was about to break into. These weren't just any old potioners—if Kyra did say so herself—but rather the most highly esteemed in the kingdom, sought out by even the king himself. Their specialty was poisonous weaponry, and they not only manufactured the weapons, they knew how to use them. Better than anyone else around.

The rough, sun-warmed shingles that sided the house were perfect for climbing, and the nearest village was a good twenty-minute walk away. It wasn't like anyone was going to *see* her. Almost no one was home.

The families were out to work and school in the village; the potioners, she assumed, were out hunting Kyra. And the hermit—well, he never went anywhere, anyway.

Kyra hoped he stayed put behind his papered-up windows

and didn't go tromping outside on one of his rare outings. Even a hermit would likely be bothered by the sight of a young woman dressed entirely in black clinging to the side of a house.

Kyra's left hand cramped as she reached for the next shingle. What she wouldn't give for a sturdy length of rope to climb. She cursed quietly. What was she doing wishing for rope? If she was going to wish for something, it should be something really important.

Like pie.

Warm from the oven, all crispy, crackly crust and oozing, juicy berries.

All of this hiding and skulking about was going to her head.

There were *other* things on her wish list—some of them even more important than pie.

At last reaching the window, Kyra pulled herself onto the ledge, flattened her body, and slid through, rolling to the floor and springing to her feet.

It was eerily quiet. She half wished Ellie the hermit would make a sound. Move a piece of furniture or something.

Kyra automatically checked her weapons. Slim holsters on her legs contained several dozen of her signature six-inch-long throwing needles, each tipped with poison.

The outside of the holsters held weapons of a different kind—special pockets of poison that no one knew about but Kyra. People had seen the effects, of course; and a mystique had built up around Kyra's ability to take out combatants with a mere breath. One tap of her palms against her holsters

and she had a fistful of poison to blow into the face of anyone who tried to take her on.

It was extremely effective. Especially at close range.

Her weapons in order, Kyra scanned the apartment. Three bedrooms to her left in various states of lived-in-ness. In front of her, the potions lab, the vials and burners empty and cold. She had a wistful moment as she breathed in the familiar alkaline stink of the lab, but it gave way to irritation when she saw that whoever had last used the beakers and dishes and retorts hadn't cleaned them. "Ned," she muttered.

To the right was the kitchen, but . . .

Not a speck of food left out.

She ignored the pangs of hunger she felt. Directly in front of her was the treasure she'd come for: the potions cabinet. Inside the glass doors were shelves of bottles in every color in the rainbow, glittering in the sunlight.

Kyra opened the large cupboard door and rifled through the bottles. Each potion was part of a numbered system. Charm potions were in the 01 series, glamour potions 02, and so on. What she was looking for was in the 07 series.

Although she could certainly use that cloaking potion with the spray top.

Kyra dropped the bottle into the small bag tied at the side of her waist.

She had to focus and not get distracted by all of the potions she'd like to steal away. She was here to get a very special potion, one that had yet to be recreated by any other potions maker.

 4

Kyra found the 07 series and picked her way through the smooth glass bottles.

It wasn't there.

She stepped back and grasped the cupboard door. It *had* to be here.

Methodically, she examined every bottle on every shelf, starting with the 01 series. The light in the room shifted slowly as the sun moved across the sky.

Nothing.

A shiver of unease ran through her. Where was it?

She was going to have to check the rest of the rooms.

Hunting for the glimmer of a wayward potion bottle, Kyra carefully made her way through the apartment.

Hers was the first bedroom, and it was empty. The old feather-stuffed mattress was propped up against the wall, dust bunnies clumped along the baseboard. Her old partners had certainly wasted no time in getting rid of her things.

The next bedroom was a bit of a disaster. Actually, a complete disaster.

Ned's room.

Clothes were strewn all over, draped over half-drunk bottles of home-brewed ale, a half-eaten pie in a state of decay, and who knew what else. Kyra eyed the mess, reluctant to take a step into the room for fear of putting her foot into a hidden pudding bowl or something worse, but there was nothing to be done. She kicked her way through the rubbish, hunting for a stray shimmer of glass.

In the dresser she found two bottles of extra-sharp ginger

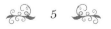

brew, lots of balled-up underwear she hoped were clean, a wedge of cheese, and a piece of paper with a clumsily drawn dancing bear announcing a show featuring animal tricks.

No potion.

Which left only the final room. Hal's.

Like him, it had an air of well-groomed arrogance. Gentlemanly cloaks worth more than a local blacksmith would make in an entire year hung neatly on hooks along the wall. The bedding was sumptuous dark velvet. Matching nightstands framed the bed.

Kyra snorted. To think she'd once been impressed by this empty gaudiness.

She went to the carved cherry dresser and yanked on the decorative iron pulls. The drawers slid out smoothly with a soft *shwep*. Inside were neatly folded clothes arranged by color.

Except.

Between folds of socks, something caught the light from the window. Something that glittered. A bit like glass.

Kyra's heart sped up.

Gingerly, she reached in and closed her fingers around the object.

It wasn't a bottle. Kyra pulled it out. A simple glass pendant dangled at the end of a chain. A woman's necklace. Had it been a gift for her before she'd broken Hal's heart?

Kyra held it up to the light coming in from the window. As she did, she caught a movement out of the corner of her eye and turned.

She almost dropped the necklace in shock when she realized what she was seeing.

Her own reflection in Hal's giant looking glass.

Kyra's heart froze in her chest.

It was the first time she'd gazed into a mirror in three months.

And she looked awful.

Her long hair was a black tangle around her face, her skin so pale it was as though the sun had turned its back on the person Kyra had become. Her collarbones jutted out the top of her black clothing. And below that . . .

She hadn't thought her chest could get any smaller, but lo and behold, her onetime skintight clothing was actually baggy across the front.

That's what going hungry did to a body.

But that wasn't even the most appalling thing.

Her eyes. They were the same olive-colored eyes she'd seen in the mirror her entire life, but different, somehow. They'd been changed by those horrible things she wished she'd never seen. They looked . . . *old*.

She looked old.

Kyra needed to get a grip. The first sixteen years of her life she'd managed not to worry about how she looked. There was no reason to start now.

She turned away from the mirror.

Then she heard the worst possible sound in the world: the downstairs door being thrown open. Followed by a loud, booming laugh.

She knew that laugh. Ned.

Kyra dashed out of the bedroom, panic rippling across her skin. She couldn't hide in the potioners' apartment; it was too risky. She could go out the window, but what if Hal was waiting outside? He'd be right there to catch her.

She opened the apartment door and stood silent on the landing, still clutching the necklace in her hand.

The booming laugh grew closer, was coming up the stairs.

Ellie's flat. Maybe she could sneak in there and hide without his seeing.

She gently closed the door behind her, threw the pendant chain around her neck, and crossed to the hermit's apartment.

Grabbing a fistful of a Release potion from her belt, she quickly blew the powder into the lock. Then the mechanisms gave way and she was in. She shut the door behind her and stood in the quiet dark, letting her eyes adjust. The covered windows let in small slits of light where cracks had formed in the paper. She could see the entire apartment from where she stood. The place was mostly empty. Some moldy-looking furniture Kyra would rather burn than sit in. And dust. Everywhere.

There was no sign of Ellie the hermit.

She hadn't seen him leave the whole week she'd staked out the place. Where could he be?

Loud footsteps tramped up the stairs and into the potioners' lodgings, accompanied by hooting laughs. Damn Ned and Hal. They weren't supposed to be home. They were supposed to be out looking for her. Why could they never be where they were supposed to be? And what was so funny, anyway?

Ellie's windows were nailed shut. Of course. And it was impossible to sneak out the front door—the wards would catch Kyra going out as well as in.

Back at Ellie's front door, Kyra got down on her hands and knees to peer through the crack at the bottom, the pendant on the necklace coming to rest on the floor beneath her. The Master Potioners' door across the hall was shut.

Kyra closed her eyes. This wasn't going very well. She hadn't gotten the potion, and she was trapped in a hermitless hermit home.

Plus, she'd just discovered that she looked old.

Fuh.

She turned away and laid her cheek to the floor. Through the floorboards she felt the buzzing of a steady stream of talk from across the landing.

Kyra opened her eyes, her face pointed toward the saggy couch. Under the couch was the glint of something.

She scooched over, curious to see what it was, and reached under, sweeping her hand around until at last she could grab it.

It was a small potion bottle, the blue phosphorescent liquid inside glowing in the dim room. On the label, printed neatly in her own tiny, cramped handwriting, was 07 211. A red skull signifying the solution's potency was in one corner, and the Master Trio's *M3* was stamped in the other.

The potion she'd been looking for.

What was it doing here?

Ellie the hermit had lived at Newman House far longer than Kyra or the other potioners, longer even than the tenants below. In all that time, he'd never done anything to even slightly draw their attention. Old Ellie the hermit kept himself to himself.

And yet he'd disappeared and left behind one of the trio's poisons. *Strange.*

The door across the hall creaked opened. Stashing the potion in the small bag above her hip, Kyra jumped up and listened carefully at the hermit's door. Footsteps went down, the front door shut, and the house was silent again.

She waited ten long beats before charging across the hall into the potioners' flat.

Only to find One of Them. Ned.

He was coming out of the messy bedroom, shoving a piece of pie into his mouth while attempting to tie the drawstring on a bag. Of course *he* had pie. It was probably warm and fresh too. His chin wobbled as he turned at the sound of the opening door.

Thwip. Thwip.

Kyra's throwing needles struck him—one in the shoulder and one in his overly large belly.

He fell without a sound. She lunged forward and caught him, and gently lowered him to the floor.

"Oh, for crying out loud," a voice came from just outside the half-open door. "What is the holdu—"

Hal's voice stopped suddenly. Kyra ignored the pang she felt, spun around, and blew into his handsome face.

His exquisite features went from surprised to blank. His bright blue eyes closed, and his black hair fell across his forehead as he slowly crumpled.

"Sorry, Hal," Kyra said as she eased him to the floor. "We always hurt the ones we don't quite love."

Hal and Ned were two of the best poisonous weapons users in the kingdom.

But Kyra was better.

She stepped over gorgeous Hal and into the hall. In less than an hour they'd both be awake and after her. The sleeping draft she favored in her weapons, Doze, was extremely effective, but short-lived.

Kyra hurtled down the stairs toward the front door. The magic wards wouldn't tell them anything they didn't already know.

She'd been here.

Out the door and into the forest she ran. She found her satchel where she had hidden it in the weeds, and slung it over her shoulder. At the edge of the forest she couldn't help but look back one last time at the home of the Master Trio of Potioners. It was run-down and seedy, yes, but it *had* been her home—where she'd made a name for herself, fallen in love with the wrong man, and betrayed everyone she'd ever known.

Back before she'd tried to murder the princess.

Two

It wasn't that Kyra didn't like the princess.

She did. Immensely.

She and Princess Ariana had been best friends since way back before Kyra had become one of the Master Trio of Potioners, back when she was just a first-year apprentice who'd been paired with Ariana as part of the princess's education. Princess Ariana had been born sickly, and the queen had hidden her away from the court to be nurtured and kept safe. Few people had ever met her, and most had only just caught brief glimpses of the girl at court functions. The princess was, after all, the heir to the entire Kingdom of Mohr, and her health couldn't be risked for anything.

But after twelve years, the queen's sister, the Duchess

Genria, had put her foot down. The princess was going to be the ruling monarch one day, and she couldn't be hidden away forever.

The queen reluctantly agreed.

Kyra had a skillful hand at cosmetic potions and charms, and it was decided that she would instruct the princess in the simple arts of makeup. If the two twelve-year-old girls became friends in the process—well, all the better. The princess needed all of the socializing she could get.

Kyra hadn't looked forward to these "lessons" at all—she despised cosmetic potions and charms—but even at twelve, she knew better than to refuse the queen.

And so one summer morning, in the enormous palace overlooking the capital city of Wexford, the queen and her sister had pushed Kyra into the princess's high-ceilinged bedroom.

To one side was a canopy bed with voluptuous ivory curtains tied back with tight, crisp ribbons at each corner, a large closet filled with stiff dresses, and a mirrored dressing table crowded in perfume bottles with unbroken wax seals. To the other side was a sitting area with stuffed chairs in front of a huge fireplace—complete with steaming tea and snacks on a little round table.

The princess sat on the floor by the table, shoving a torn bit of bun into her mouth.

"Ariana," the queen announced, "you have company. Do you feel well enough for a visit?"

Princess Ariana industriously plucked currants out of the remaining bun.

She looked perfectly healthy to Kyra. Bored, maybe—but that had certainly never killed anyone.

The duchess gave the queen a sister-to-sister *come on, you can do it* look, and the queen visibly steeled herself. "Ariana. Come here." Her tone had changed to the one she used to issue decrees.

Ariana got up and made her way over, a crumb stuck to the side of her cheek.

"This is Kyra," the duchess said. "She knows makeup and more. You two are going to learn so *much* from each other." She took the queen's elbow, her green eyes sparkling. "Let's leave them alone, Your Highness. They certainly don't need us."

With one last look at her daughter, the queen let the duchess lead her out of the room.

The door whispered shut and Kyra was alone with the princess.

The two girls stared defiantly at each other across the middle of the spacious room.

"I'm not interested in being beautiful," Princess Ariana said, pressing her lips together so tightly they grew as white as her skin. Her hideous robin's-egg-blue dress poufed out around her legs and arms, but the bodice was so tight it was a wonder she could breathe. Even her hair had been bound into tight gold ringlets around her head. She looked extremely uncomfortable.

"Great. Because I'm not interested in making you beautiful." Kyra set her potions trunk on the floor.

She was thankful for her practical potions-apprentice garb—the dark cloth was loose and flexible and would withstand just about anything she could do to it in the course of her studies. But over her protests, the dark waves of her hair had been brushed smooth—the duchess had insisted Kyra at least *try* to look presentable for the young heir to the throne.

The duchess had a bewitching way of looking at you that made you feel grubby-faced and wanting, followed by an immediate desire to please. Kyra had fought the urge to obey her—she had a mind of her own, thank you very much—and yet . . . she *had* scrubbed herself to within an inch of her life.

The princess turned her back on Kyra in a loud swish of skirts and walked to one of the tall arched windows that lit the room in skinny patches of sunlight.

Kyra shrugged. It wasn't like she didn't have enough unfinished homework for her apprenticeship. She had plenty she could be doing.

And she wasn't one to waste time.

Kyra snapped open the brass clasps of her leather trunk and pulled out her recording notebook. She had a potion due the following morning. Donning her protective gloves, goggles, and apron, she spread a plush black fabric across the parquet floor and set her trunk on top of it. The potion she was working on was completely inert, but hours of Safe Practice lessons had been drilled into her.

A glass tube contained her homework—a clear liquid with tiny rectangular flecks of gold floating in it.

Carefully, she uncorked it and set it in her work rack.

Levity 062, the final ingredient, was a wispy substance. She used long skinny pincers to pull out a tuft from a vial and dropped it into the gold-flecked liquid. Swirling her potion around with her left hand, she put the bottle of Levity away with her right, then held the test tube up to the sunlight streaming through the windows. The rectangular flecks were beginning to bow up at the ends into shimmering gold smiles.

Kyra's own mouth turned up in response.

Perfect. She scribbled down her final notes, the muslin-wrapped stick of writing graphite smudging across the page in her haste. Then she began adding up all of the components to get the final number for her potion.

"What's that?" a loud voice said in her left ear.

Kyra nearly dropped the potion, but caught herself just in time and said casually, "Nothing you'd be interested in, I'm sure." She didn't look at the princess but continued with her calculations, at last transferring the final potion number onto the tube's label with an ink-dipped pen.

"How is anyone going to read *that*?" the princess demanded, eying Kyra's tiny, cramped writing.

Kyra turned abruptly toward her. "Would you like to try it out?"

The princess's eyes widened.

"It won't hurt." Kyra put the bottle of ink and her pen back inside the box. What was she doing? The last thing she needed was to get into a mess if the princess reacted badly. Not that Kyra doubted her work; she was sure the potion was fine. But if it got back to the duchess that she'd experimented on the princess with a homework lesson . . . well, she would be in huge trouble.

Princess Ariana defiantly crossed her arms and said, "I'm not afraid of some silly potion."

Kyra caught a little wobble in her voice.

"I've met *lots* of potioners," the princess went on. "A bunch of toady old men in smelly robes who claimed to be healers. But their potions never did much of anything for me."

"Maybe that's because you aren't really sick." Kyra was shocked at her own words, and immediately wished she could take them back. It was the sort of thing that was whispered by court gossips. But never to the princess herself.

Princess Ariana's mouth hung open, but she didn't say anything, so Kyra forged ahead. "Anyway, I'm not going to become a healing potioner. I'm interested in *much* more exciting things." She picked a small dropper out of her trunk. "Put out your hand."

Apparently, Kyra had shocked Ariana beyond resistance. She obeyed, her fingers trembling only slightly. "I met a witch once too," Ariana said in a rush of nerves. "Stupid old hag tied string around my hands, dumped powder on me, and told a bunch of silly stories about curses and spells and make-believe monsters like obeekas, who change shapes and suck out souls—"

"I've never heard of those and I'm studying magical creatures."

"—and about witches in the south who can stop a person in their tracks with the evil eye, and how birds called grecks suck out people's brains, and about the gortha mice who run over their prey like water and eat 'em alive, and—"

"Be quiet," Kyra said, lowering the head of the dropper into the potion tube. "I'm trying to concentrate."

The princess was silent for a moment. "You know," she went on in a whisper, "witches are different from other people. Some say they aren't even human."

Kyra's stomach tightened. This was the kind of talk that led to houses being burnt down and all manner of atrocities. It wasn't that Kyra was fond of witches—they hadn't earned their nasty reputations for nothing—but she couldn't stand violence against people because of something that they had no control over. Witches never had a choice: they were born the way they were, just as people didn't get to choose which family they were born into. "They're human, all right," she said.

"That's not what Nurse told me," the princess said defiantly. "She wasn't happy about them bringing the witch in at all—what would people say?"

"I'd be less worried about what people said and more worried about the witch's magic going wrong," Kyra responded. "Witchcraft is completely unscientific."

She filled the dropper with her potion, maneuvered it over the princess's hand, and squeezed out one single bead of liquid. It fell with a plop on Ariana's pale white skin.

The two girls waited, their conversation forgotten.

And then a small giggle erupted from the princess. She looked surprised at the sound coming out of her own mouth.

Kyra had the horrible impression that giggling was probably an unusual occurrence in the princess's life.

"What is it?" Ariana asked, chortling freely now. "I've never felt anything like it."

"A laughing potion," Kyra said. "I gave you enough for about five minutes."

Ariana grabbed her belly, rolled around on the floor, and hooted.

Kyra couldn't help but smile.

After the laughter had settled down to hiccups, Ariana grabbed Kyra's arm. "I had no idea. I never dreamed potions could work so well." She swallowed a hiccup and started laughing again. "Or be so much fun."

Her eyes flitted to the window. The bright blue day beckoned from beyond the glass.

"I don't suppose . . ." she began, grabbing a fistful of skirt and twisting it around her fist. "I don't suppose you could make something to get us out of here?"

"Definitely." Kyra's mind ran through her options. She could do this. It was just a matter of putting her knowledge to work. But she had to do it with what was available in her trunk.

She got out a piece of chalk and drew a circle around herself and her potions trunk. "You have to stay on that side of the line," she said, pointing to the far side.

"Okay." The princess eyed the chalk line suspiciously. "I'm not scared."

"Ariana, you should be." Kyra realized the second after

she said it that she probably should have asked to use the princess's name first, but it was too late now. "The laughing potion was completely safe, but if we're going to sneak out of here, we're going to need something a little more dangerous. I'm a trained potions apprentice, but *you* need to stay outside the circle, where it's safe." She didn't mention that the potion she'd be creating was way above her level of training.

Ariana nodded reluctantly but stayed put.

Kyra lifted out the top tray of the trunk—all lower-numbered potions used for cosmetics and charms—and went straight to the bottom layer, where she had higher-numbered potions. The 05 series through the 07.

The poisons.

Poisons were fatal at full strength, but diluted correctly, they were usually completely safe. Or almost always. And you could do amazing things with them that you couldn't do with the lower-numbered benign potions.

Kyra needed to dilute the poisons by just the right amount. If the solution was too weak, the mixture wouldn't do what she wanted; but if it wasn't diluted enough, it would kill her and the princess pretty much on the spot.

She filled a vial three-quarters of the way up with dilution elixir, then squeezed in one drop of a confusion poison and two drops of a concealment poison. Next she sprinkled in a pinch of a lower-numbered glamour dust, screwed on the cap, and shook the whole thing.

Taking a deep breath, she dampened a cloth with the solution and dabbed herself and her clothes all over while the princess watched, her pale blue eyes intense.

This was it. Either Kyra would die from extreme confusion, die from disappearing into nothingness . . . or live and be extremely difficult to see.

"Kyra?" Ariana's voice was filled with wonder. "I think it worked."

Kyra looked down at herself.

She most certainly was difficult to see. She sort of blended into the background.

Perfect.

Kyra quickly packed up her kit, but not quick enough to keep Ariana from bouncing foot to foot and babbling, "Let's go, let's go, let's go!"

"Okay, okay!" Kyra laughed at her. "You're sure you're ready?"

Ariana stopped bouncing and shot her an evil look.

"Ouch. I guess you're ready." She stepped out of the chalk circle. "You know, you really shouldn't give such a hard time to the hardworking potioner who's going to break you out of jail."

"You're right," Princess Ariana said, and swept a huge curtsy. "You are my champion."

Kyra rolled her eyes and started dabbing the princess all over with the handkerchief.

In a meadow full of sunshine, the girls fell into a giggling heap on the ground. They were outside the castle, an hour's walk from the city. The cloaking potion was wearing off.

Princess Ariana's face split into a beatific smile as she held out her arms to the sun. "This is the best thing that's ever happened to me in my whole entire life," she said. "I don't even know where to start. We can do *anything*."

"Well, not anything," Kyra said. "We don't want to get caught."

"But that still leaves so many options." Princess Ariana rolled over on one elbow and looked serious. "Have you ever tipped a cow?"

"What?" Kyra brushed a leaf out of her hair.

"My nanny says she used to do it a million years ago when she was a kid. When the cows are napping you push them and they fall right over. It doesn't hurt or anything, just confuses them, I think."

"Why in the world would anyone want to tip a cow?"

"I don't know, but there's only one way to find out." Princess Ariana jumped up and started running in the direction of a barn in the next field over.

"You can't be serious. Right? Right, Ariana?"

Kyra ran after her.

Kyra and Ariana's weekly "lessons" turned into secret adventures in the countryside, the two girls stealing out of the castle using Kyra's potion. Their friendship blossomed, and over the next five years, Ariana became the best friend Kyra would probably ever have.

Which was why it had been such a shock to everyone when, three months ago, Kyra had tried to kill her.

And failed, Kyra reminded herself now as she tramped through the woods.

Thinking about Ariana made her heart ache. And Kyra

had resolved not to let that happen. She'd spent the last several months diligently hardening her heart. She couldn't allow one tiny crack.

Or she would fall apart.

The princess had to die. It was either her or the rest of the kingdom.

But first Kyra had to *find* the princess.

Her satchel slung over her shoulder, the necklace she'd accidentally stolen bouncing around her neck, Kyra made her way quickly through the woods. To either side of her, the bright spring buds of leafing trees stood out against the long dark skirts of pines.

She wended her way into the overgrown hollow to the gigantic oak tree that marked her hideaway. Kyra sprinkled the antidote concoction on the ground in front of her until a section of concealment faded away and the entrance to her hut became visible.

Kyra stepped inside. The hut smelled of earth, iron, oils, and cleaning solutions. Light from the one perfectly square window lit up the tiny room.

On the far wall hung weapons of every size and shape—a half dozen swords whose edges glowed with deadly potions; sharp curving machetes; dirks and bodkins and all manner of small knives in holsters; and maces and morning stars prickly with wicked-looking spikes. A sizable wooden chest on one side of the room doubled as a table.

Shortly after the Master Trio of Potioners had moved into the apartment at Newman House, Kyra realized she was going to need a place of her own, a secret place to get away

from the very maleness of Hal and Ned.

She'd learned carpentry from a woodworker at the castle, and she'd built the hut all by herself with the skills she'd picked up. Not a single crack of light came in through the tightly fitted boards. No one but Kyra and her best friend, Ariana, knew of the hut's existence.

She would be sorry to leave it but knew it was time to say good-bye.

Kyra added a brace of throwing quills and two small daggers to her pack, grabbed her bedroll and the last of her food—a stale half loaf of bread and a hard wedge of cheese—then shut the door firmly behind her. She closed the opening she'd made in the concealment charm and set out over the slippery pine needles that covered the forest floor.

Ned and Hal would be awake soon. They'd be hunting for Kyra now that they knew she wasn't very far away.

But they'd never expect her to seek help from the most villainous character in the kingdom. No one in their right mind purposely sought out Arlo Abbaduto.

He and Kyra went way back. She had crossed him previously on two different occasions, and sincerely wished she hadn't. Both times before, the King of Criminals had come to her, not the other way around. She'd had the upper hand those times. But now she'd be on his territory. In his power.

And there was nowhere else to turn for help.

By the time the sun began to sink below the treetops and the spring air turned cool, Kyra had put several good miles between herself and her old home. She didn't know these woods and didn't want to fend for herself after dark. She had to find Arlo's lair soon.

She knew it was in the forest east of Tippolow. That was all. But she hadn't come across anything even remotely resembling a crook's hideout. It didn't help that she had no idea what she was looking for. What sort of residence would the monstrously vain King of Criminals go for? Something enormous and shiny would fit his giant ego, but something hidden, dank, and dark would probably be more likely.

And harder to find.

Pink fingers of sunset lit the sky as she watched the lights of Tippolow appear in the distance. Skirting the forest's edge, she went still farther north until she could no longer see any sign of the town. No luck.

She turned to head back and almost tripped over a boy and a girl who'd been following close on her heels.

"Hey!" she said, startled. "You should watch where you're going!"

They stared up at her with black midnight eyes.

Unblinking.

Three

"HI," KYRA SAID, squeezing her eyes shut for a moment. Looking at the children made her skin crawl.

She didn't like children at the best of times, and now was certainly nowhere near the best of times. It was even possibly the worst of times, though Kyra kept thinking she'd hit bottom only to discover that things could still get worse. She opened her eyes.

The children silently continued to stare up at her.

They had freaky eyes and were unnaturally alike—much more so than any normal twins she'd ever seen. The only thing distinguishing one from the other was that the girl's hair was in pigtails. "Here's the thing. I know you're probably lost and need help, but I really don't have time to go hunting for your mummy and daddy, sorry. Tippolow is back that way just a bit." Kyra gestured in the direction of town. "I'm sure someone there will help you." She turned away only to find that one of them was again in front her. The boy.

Where there had been no child before.

Creepy.

Kyra sidestepped him. "I'm in a bit of a hurry."

The girl came up beside her and took her arm.

Kyra tried to politely brush her off. "No, really."

The girl's fingers tightened.

Soon the boy was on her other arm.

Their grip was absurdly strong for children.

Unless they weren't children at all. One smiled up at her, and Kyra saw that his eyes weren't just dark—they were completely black, with no whites.

Kyra threw herself to the ground, and when the boy creature lost his hold, she slapped her palm against her holster and blew her Doze potion into his face. Some sleep certainly wouldn't hurt him. Whatever he was.

He stared, long eyelashes framing his black eyes. Then he reached for her arm once more. Kyra dodged him and tried blowing again, but it had no effect.

This had never happened before. Doze was effective on all kinds of human creatures. What were these children that they weren't affected?

The boy took Kyra's arm again, and he and his sister yanked her through a stand of dead pines, onto a muddy path that bordered a foul-smelling swamp. Up ahead was a giant mound of earth.

A hidden entrance led to a tunnel. Torches lined the walls, and the shadows cast by Kyra's tiny captors stretched like those of gigantic monsters. It was only a trick of the light, but it sent a shiver right through Kyra. Their touch left her strangely weak.

At the end of the tunnel, a large sulfurous cavern bustled with activity. Hammers clanged, men grunted at their work, and wheelbarrows loaded with metal scraps went to a huge red glowing vat and came away empty. There were trolls lifting giant crates, and goblins sharpening weapons. At the center of it all, shouting at a group of oversized thugs and ratty-looking thieves, was the unmistakable hulking form of Arlo Abbaduto. His gigantic head was completely hairless, leaving nothing to distract from his misshapen nose and freakish protruding eyes.

Great. Yes, she'd wanted to meet with Arlo—King of Criminals, Master of Thieves, Ruler of Wrongdoers, and so forth—but not *this* way, not frog-marched in by two evil little munchkins, their tiny fingers clamped down so hard Kyra could feel her arms bruising.

As she was led past a group of gnarled old women, the hairs on the back of her neck prickled. *Witches.* One caught Kyra's eye and stared hard until Kyra felt she was drowning in the hag's milky gray gaze.

Kyra's vision clouded, and in her mind's eye was a kitchen garden festering with rot. Tomatoes sagged on withered stems, coneflowers bowed under the weight of blight, and desiccated herbs blew away in a hot dead breeze.

Kyra squeezed her eyes shut and shook away the images.

 28

She kept her eyes averted until the witches were far behind her. It wouldn't do to reveal too much here, in the lair of the king of thieves.

When Kyra and the munchkins came into his line of sight, Arlo fell quiet.

Recognition spread across his round face.

"Well, well, well," he said. "What have we here? Is the Princess Killer herself deigning to grace us with her presence?"

The men around them scuttled off.

Kyra's cheeks warmed. She jerked her arms from her tiny captors, feeling a surge of renewed vigor as their fingers broke away from her. "I didn't kill the princess."

"But you tried. And you were *so* close." Arlo put his pudgy fingers an inch apart to illustrate his point. "Rumor has it you were her best friend too? Beautiful." He slowly blinked his bulbous eyes. "How low the mighty have fallen, *Master Potioner*." He mock-bowed to her, unfurling his fat arm with a flourish.

The Master Trio of Potioners had been together less than a year when Arlo had visited. He came in person, a rare honor. He'd wanted some particularly sensitive poisons, and he was willing to pay handsomely.

They'd turned him down cold. They'd been so proud. Hal in his velvet cloak, his shiny riding boots propped up on the table; Ned with his hands crossed in satisfaction over his fat belly; and Kyra . . . It killed her to remember the haughty look she'd given the King of Criminals, and the disdainful way she'd said, "Why would we help the likes of *you*?" as though he were a piece of garbage in the street.

That was the first time she'd met him. The second time, she behaved even worse.

She didn't want to think about that. She shook herself out of the memory and said, "Look, I came here to do business with you."

"You did?" He looked pointedly at the children on either side of her. "It looks to me like you came here as a prisoner."

One of her freaky little captors opened his mouth, large dark eyes glittering. "We brought you another slave, Your Majesty. Don't you think she'll clean up nice?" His voice was far deeper and fuller than Kyra would have expected. It sounded magnified, like many low voices at once.

"Oh," Arlo said, "my little friends, you've brought me something far better than just a mere slave. This one's talents are . . . extensive."

Kyra was *not* going to become a slave. No way.

While the children bowed to Arlo, acknowledging his praise, she shoved the boy face-first into the ground and leapfrogged over him onto one of the wooden crates. Her back to the wall, she pulled a throwing needle and aimed it directly at Arlo's heart. "They might be immune to my poison, but you aren't."

The child creature she'd pushed stood up and glared, seeming to grow bigger as his eyes bored into her.

Arlo put his hands up in front of him. "Settle down." He jerked his head at the kids. "You two, scram."

With one last scowl at Kyra, they left, the boy rubbing his face with his hand.

"I don't want to fight you," Arlo said.

Kyra watched him, the needle still raised. "Are you going to help me?"

"Why," he asked, lids half lowered, "should I do that?"

"You know how deadly my poisons are." She stared him down. "Would you like to test my aim?"

"What exactly is it that you want?" the King of Criminals said.

"I need to find someone, and I know you have . . . ways of finding people." Kyra jumped down from the box, keeping her needle at the ready.

"Why would someone as exalted as a *Master Potioner* need the aid of a lowly king of thieves? I was under the impression that I was beneath your notice. Surely a potioner of your standing has her own ways of finding people."

The last thing Kyra wanted was to admit the shortcomings of potions work. People generally had the idea that potioners could do just about anything, but their magic was limited. Only one known potion could be used to track people, and it had to be applied directly to the subject beforehand. Not the most useful of charms.

Kyra lowered her throwing arm as a sign of trust. She was quick enough to nail Arlo before he could attack her. Even with her arm down. "I don't have any other options."

Kyra wished she didn't sound quite so desperate. Hell, she wished she *wasn't* so desperate. But after Kyra's failed assassination attempt on the princess's sixteenth birthday, Ariana had completely disappeared. Kyra had spent the last three months hunting for the princess but had learned very little.

All the while, Kyra had been evading capture, living on

the fringes of towns, using glamours, confusion potions, and all manner of deceit to disguise herself.

Because if the authorities caught her, she would hang.

Arlo seemed to enjoy having Kyra at his mercy. A hideous grin spread across his wide face. If anything, it made him uglier.

"And what"—his monstrous eyes swept across her body—"do you have to offer me in return?"

"I don't have access to a potions lab the way I used to."

"I know," Arlo said. "That wasn't what I had in mind at all. Though I'm sure we could find some raw materials for you to tinker with."

"I have money," Kyra said, reaching for her satchel.

"So do I." Arlo grinned wider, his lips parting and revealing masses of mossy teeth.

"But do you have any of these?" She pulled out a pouch and loosened the drawstring. An eerie green glowed from within.

"Potioners' coins." Arlo's voice sounded impressed despite himself.

Kyra shook one into his huge hand. He held it up to his eye. "These could come in handy."

Kyra didn't doubt they would be useful for someone as crooked as Arlo. Potioners' coins looked like regular coins to the naked eye, but no matter where they were spent, they always ended up back in their owner's pockets.

"And you'll change their owner imprint to me?"

"Of course."

"I just might have something for you, then." Arlo gestured for Kyra to follow. He led her deep into the cavern. She walked behind him, keeping her guard up through the dark halls. The air grew more and more noxious, until Kyra felt like she was trapped in an unshoveled barn.

She saw the shadowy movement of animals she couldn't identify.

"Here." Arlo opened an iron gate near the end of the cavern.

Inside was one small pink pig. About the size of a house cat.

"Are you kidding me?" Kyra liked animals just about as much as she liked children.

"It's a Katzenheim pig. Best hunter we've got. She'll find the person you're looking for."

Kyra looked down at the little creature. It had perked up at the sound of their voices and lifted its head to look at them in what Kyra could only describe as a hopeful way. It wasn't that she'd never heard of Katzenheim pigs, but more as the punch line to a joke than as an actual practical means to finding someone. The idea of trusting her mission to a pig seemed borderline insane. Before Kyra could open her mouth to protest, Arlo had placed the pig's leash in her hand and started down the hall.

"Hey!" she shouted after him, then scurried to follow when he didn't turn back. The pig trotted amiably beside her.

Kyra caught up to Arlo as he turned off into a giant storeroom piled high with what Kyra could only guess were stolen objects. There were crystal vases, fine china, women's lacy shawls, jewels tumbling out of cases, a stuffed stag's head with one marble eye popped out, bolts of silk and satin, oil lamps with half-burned wicks, and more—too much more to see at a glance.

"This really wasn't what I had in mind," Kyra said to the back of Arlo's oversized head.

He grunted and kept going.

She stepped closer to one of the shelves to get a better look at the bust of what appeared to be a military general, but jerked back when she realized it wasn't a statue. It was a real head.

If she needed to be reminded of who she was dealing with, Mr. Dead Frozen Head had done it. She wasn't just working with a criminal—she was working with a monstrous one.

Kyra shook herself.

Leaving there with a pig was starting to seem like an almost sensible idea.

"How is this pig supposed to find who I'm looking for?" she couldn't help asking Arlo as he poked around on the shelves in front of her.

"That is what this is for." He pulled a tiny basket down from a shelf. "You put an object belonging to the person into the basket, put it around the pig's neck, and you'll have no problem finding *whomever* you're looking for."

He pulled a small scarf out of a bin, lifted the lid of the basket, and shoved the material inside. "Lucky for you, I just happen to have something belonging to *whomever*." He winked at her. "Always happy to help damage the kingdom."

"I'm not—"

"Give Her Highness my best. Or not." Arlo's thunderous laugh echoed throughout the cavern.

Four

KYRA LEANED BACK INTO the crook of the tree trunk, her long hair catching on the bark as she settled in. Darkness surrounded her and stars peeked through the silhouette of the upper branches of the tree.

Before laying out her bedroll, she'd placed potion wards in a perimeter around the tree to alert her to anyone approaching. Making a concealment charm from scratch would have been too much work for a one-night stay.

She knew it didn't offer much protection, but it felt good to have a large tree against her back. The pig certainly wasn't going to be much use in a fight.

The pig.

It was the most ridiculous thing in the entire world: Kyra, would-be assassin and master potioner, had resorted to hunting down her prey—her best friend the princess—with a piglet.

But she had no choice. The princess had to die.

Didn't she?

A twist of doubt swirled through Kyra. What if she was wrong?

The pig tucked itself up next to her, grunting contentedly. Kyra had fed it a chunk of her stale bread as she'd laid out her bedroll, then taken a handful for herself before wrapping it up. Another mouth to feed. Kyra had a hard enough time getting food for herself!

She pushed the pig away, along with her doubts about her mission. It had been a long day and she felt bruised inside by her encounter with Ned and Hal. Gently, she lifted the necklace out of her shirt—and gasped.

It glowed in the dark. Like a tiny oblong moon dangling from a chain.

Well! That might be useful.

She reached into her satchel, pulled out the soft velvet of her potions bag, and picked through a handful of the glass vials, the necklace lighting up the tiny print on the labels. There was the cloaking potion in its special misting bottle; her signature sleeping potion, Doze, which she used to tip her needles; a tracking potion—which was almost completely useless; and a couple of glamours for use as disguises. Each went back into the bag with a gentle clink.

Aha. The potion she was looking for: 07 211, otherwise known as Peccant Pentothal. One of the strongest poisons in the world.

Perfect for taking out the princess.

Kyra carefully shook the vial of phosphorescent blue liquid next to her ear. A little under half full. She slipped the bottle back into the bag and tied it closed. Questions rumbled through her head.

But she wasn't going to find any answers tonight. Tonight she just needed to get some sleep. A thorough bath wouldn't hurt either, but she couldn't do anything about that at the moment.

Kyra slipped the necklace back under her shirt to hide the light. There were people hunting for her, after all. No need to draw their attention.

She slumped farther down into her bedroll, pushing thoughts of being hunted and the dark creatures of the world to the back of her mind. Kyra wasn't just tired. She was completely exhausted. The pig wormed its way back over and was resting against her leg.

Kyra discovered she was actually too tired to push it away.

At least it didn't smell.

Kyra woke up the next morning with the feeling that something was wrong. She was stiff and cold and there was a weight on her chest that didn't belong there. It felt warm and . . . *alive*. Her eyes flew open, expecting to see that a soul-sucking succubus had somehow made it through her defenses.

But it was just a tiny pig.

The pig. *Right.*

Kyra rubbed her eyes and sat up, dislodging the pig as she did so.

She grabbed her pack and opened the top.

Her spare clothes were identical to the ones she was wearing. Her standard black outfit was practical and low-key. Perfect for the road. The spare set had several good wears before needing a wash.

But underthings were a whole different story. She was down to one last clean pair.

Worse, this last pair of clean underthings was a complete joke. Not only were they the most ridiculous, feminine, beribboned bit of foolishness that ever existed, but they'd been a gift from Princess Ariana.

Ariana had specially commissioned them for Kyra's sixteenth birthday the fall before, and she'd embroidered them herself. In none-too-neat stitching, the word KITTY—Ariana's nickname for Kyra—was written across the left bosom of the waist-length shift. On the right was a horrible image of a cat. It appeared to be winking. Or suffering some sort of nervous facial tic. And the lower half was almost worse—cut off high on the thigh and festooned with ruffles all across the bottom.

By the time Ariana turned fifteen, it was undeniably clear that she was no longer ill. She bloomed with health, and her temper had taken a sharp turn for the better. Ariana had grown to be a large-boned gangly teen with a splash of freckles across her face, her neat ringlets replaced by a wild mane of frizz that suited her perfectly. A girl who didn't eat her tea biscuits daintily, but instead crushed them up into crumbs to feed the birds on her parapet.

It wasn't ladylike. So the queen brought in a group of well-bred girls to be her ladies-in-waiting and insisted Ari learn a feminine craft.

Ariana chose embroidery.

The princess made the most of it, but she fit into her sewing circle about as easily as a hunting dog. Ariana was no lap puppy, and Kyra could never suppress a grin at the sight of tomboyish Ari with her ladies—the polished fine-boned girls of the kingdom with their pretty silk dresses and artfully arranged hair.

As different (and often shocking) as Ariana was, Kyra could tell that most of the ladies-in-waiting were fond of the princess. It was difficult not to get caught up in her infectious laughter.

And how she had laughed when Kyra opened her birthday gift on the first of November, shortly after Kyra had announced her engagement.

Kyra could feel the look of horror crossing her face and had quickly popped the top back on the box. Lowering her voice, she'd whispered, "Ariana! You must be *stopped*. I'm serious. Someone needs to lock you away with the other crazy people."

Ariana wiped tears of glee off her cheeks. "You know you love it, and *he's* going to love it even more." She erupted with another gale of laughter.

Kyra put her hand over Ariana's. "It's weird—we'd both sworn we'd never do anything so stupid as get married, but,

Ari, it feels right. It really does. And it isn't going to be for ages, really—not till next year."

The light still sparkled in the princess's eyes, but she looked unusually serious when she replied. "Just because *I'm* not going to ever get married doesn't mean that you can't. We'll still be best friends, right?"

"Right."

They'd been so, so wrong.

How had this underwear ended up in her pack?

Kyra's subconscious must have been out to punish her.

Granted, she'd been in a bit of a rush, what with all the soldiers in the realm hunting her down. She had a vague memory of grabbing a drawer and dumping its entire contents into her pack.

Kyra dressed quickly, thankful when the undergarments disappeared under her clothes.

She set the pig on its feet and shouldered her pack. "Okay, it's time. Do your thing, pig."

The pig didn't move. It looked up at her.

What was the problem? Did she need special words or something?

The pig kept its eyes on her. It looked like it was smiling. If pigs could smile.

For the love of all that was good in the world, it wasn't expecting breakfast, was it? Kyra liked food as much as the next person, but this was a *hunt*. Who had time for breakfast?

Kyra lifted the flap on the side pocket of her pack and pulled out a wedge of cheese. "Here." She threw it to the pig.

Scarfing up the cheese, the pig started down the trail.

The pig certainly looked like it knew where it was going. Now that it had finished breakfast, it rushed through the forest, its pink nose to the ground, oinking excitedly every so often.

Until they came to a river. The pig paced back and forth, looking up at Kyra.

She stood on the sloping bank and looked out over the rushing water.

"Great. You've led us to a RIVER, pig. This isn't helpful."

The pig oinked back at her.

Maybe seven or eight hours from now a river would be useful, but Kyra was far from ready to stop for the day to do her laundry.

She sat down on the riverbank under the drooping branches of a willow tree and tried to configure her mental map. They'd gone northwest from Arlo's and walked several miles since they'd gotten up that morning. This had to be the Iota River.

There was a major bridge to the east that crossed the Iota. It was only about fifteen miles away, but it was off the pig's chosen track. West, the river ran for miles before petering out into swamps and bogs.

They were going to have to cross the old-fashioned way—by getting wet.

At this point the Iota was only about ten yards across and shallow-looking. Kyra could even make out the river bottom through the water.

Definitely crossable—for Kyra, anyway. As she sat staring off into the water, the pig had curled itself around her shoe.

She sighed and looked down at it. "Pigs can't swim, can they?"

Kyra considered throwing it in to see if it could, but shook her head. If this pig really could do what it was supposed to, it was too valuable to risk.

"Ugh. You are such a pain."

Kyra stripped off her clothing, feeling like she was taking off a layer of armor. Her clothes had been treated with potions to repel liquids, but water still got trapped between the fabric and her skin. She'd end up having to take them off to get dry anyway.

Maybe it would have been worth a little discomfort. She was completely exposed standing on the riverbank in her undergarments, the grass prickly beneath her bare feet.

Why did she have to be wearing *these* underthings?

A breeze set the ribbons trembling. Kyra briskly rubbed her hands over her arms to warm them up and reached down to pull out the knife she had tucked into her ankle garter. She grasped one ribbon and put the blade to the base of it.

And paused.

Another puff of wind set the ribbons dancing.

She couldn't do it. She couldn't chop the ribbons off Ariana's silly gift.

Kyra sighed and arranged her clothing into a nest, the material soft beneath her fingers. She wrapped her cloth shoes in her tunic and pants, keeping her weapons holsters on the outside so she could reach them if need be.

The pig crawled right into the center of the bundle and looked up expectantly.

"Oh, I'm sure you just love this. *You're* supposed to be the worker, here. I shouldn't have to carry you around."

But there was no avoiding it. Picking up the pig and nest, she held them in front of her and stepped into the water. *Icy.*

The water got deeper until it was just below her waist and tugging at the hem of her long Kitty underwear. If it got much deeper, her things and the pig would get wet. She was going to have to balance her knapsack and the nest of pig on top of her head.

She carefully lifted the whole bundle up, still keeping her fingers protectively wrapped around her weapons.

How had she come to this? How had she ended up a hungry, friendless fugitive in the middle of a frigid river wearing completely ridiculous lacy underthings?

With a pig balanced on top of her head?

At least there was no one around.

Just as she thought that, a piercing whistle cut through her thoughts.

No. Way.

Kyra froze, her hands seizing the pig, and looked in the direction of the whistle.

A young man—he couldn't have been more than a couple of years older than she was—stood across the shore on the sandy bank, watching her appreciatively. He was dressed in rough traveling clothes, and his brown hair was rumpled like he'd just woken up.

Kyra scanned him—he didn't appear to have any weapons, his stance was open and relaxed, and he didn't bear any insignia of the militia.

"This certainly isn't something you see every day," the young man said in an accented voice. He settled himself against a big boulder three feet from the river's edge and crossed his arms as though sitting back to enjoy a show. Even from where she was, Kyra could tell he was good-looking. He held himself in that confident way good-looking guys have.

Kyra had had quite enough of handsome men to last her a lifetime.

She started walking again, moving slowly forward through the cold water—she couldn't let this jerk keep her from crossing the river. And she certainly wasn't turning back.

"This isn't something *you* should be seeing at all," she said loudly over the rushing sound of the river. "Whoever you are, I'd appreciate it if you'd leave."

"And miss this?" The boy appeared to be considering her request, his head cocked to the side as he watched. "No," he continued, "I think I'll stay. Besides, what if you slip and fall? I'll be right here to help you."

He wasn't a threat, just an annoyance. A big annoyance, but Kyra was going to have to ignore him.

Somewhat difficult to do. The current was getting stronger. Instead of crossing quickly, as she would have liked, she had to step slowly and make sure each foot had a solid hold before moving the other one.

She chanced a glance up and saw something that made her heart stop.

Just behind the young man was a wolf. It watched them with glittering eyes.

The pig noticed the wolf a second later.

 45

And went crazy.

It squealed and twisted itself around in the clothing atop Kyra's head. She tried to hold it tighter, but the pig was thrashing about so furiously it was impossible for her to get a good grip.

Kyra recoiled as one of the pig's hooves poked her in the eye.

Next thing she knew, she was under the freezing water and the pig was gone.

Swept away with all of her weapons.

Five

Kyra told herself not to panic.

She would NOT drown in water that was shallower than she was tall. She needed to find the riverbed. But just as her foot brushed the bottom, it got caught in the current and shot out from under her.

She thrashed her feet and hands out frantically to try to touch ground again, but they slid cleanly through the water without hitting anything solid.

The bottom had disappeared.

Suddenly a strong hand caught her and pulled her straight up. Air hit her face. She sucked in deep luscious breaths.

She was cradled against an extremely warm body, one that smelled tantalizingly of roasted spices and wood fire.

She looked up to see the young man gazing down at her, his face inches from her own, the corners of his eyes crinkled in concern.

"You okay?"

She nodded, not quite able to catch her breath to talk yet.

His eyes were stunning. They were a vibrant green with little flecks of amber and gold, like glimpses of the sun through a canopy of leaves. His face looked like a painting of some kind of trickster god—equal parts mischief and pleasure. Like the world had been created as his playground and he was enjoying every minute of his time here.

No one should look that pleased with life.

His lips looked so soft, Kyra wondered for a moment what it would be like to touch them, and she realized they were turned up at the corners as he caught her staring at him.

"You know," he said, "you didn't have to go to all of this trouble just to get my attention."

"Don't flatter yourself," Kyra said with all of the dignity she could muster.

He replied with a grin.

"Put me down," Kyra said.

"Really? You want me to put you down? Right now?" Kyra realized they weren't moving. "That water's awfully cold."

"On the shore." Her lungs hurt from holding her breath, her nose was raw inside, she was cold and disoriented, and she was in the most vulnerable position she'd been in in months.

The boy started toward the bank. "I don't have a ton of experience with rescuing helpless maidens, but I was under the impression they're usually a lot more grateful."

 48

"I am NOT a helpless maiden."

"You're kind of cute when you're angry, has anyone ever told you that?"

Kyra glared up at the boy.

"Yep, that's just exactly what I'm talking about."

That's when she remembered. "Where's my pig?" She struggled to look down into the water.

"Safe on the shore. I grabbed her first and then came back for you."

On the riverbank, Kyra's pig was sitting happily on the boulder. Relieved, she sagged against the boy, and a rush of sensation flooded through her. His jacket rough against her skin, the play of muscles in his chest, Kyra was suddenly very physically aware of him. She stiffened and pulled herself away as much as she could. "You saved the pig while I was drowning?"

He chuckled. "Thought she must be valuable or you wouldn't have carried her on top of your head. Besides, pigs can't swim. They cut their little throats with their sharp hooves." His arms still cradling Kyra, he demonstrated, paddling his hands under her.

Good-looking AND completely insane.

"Besides, as you said, you're no helpless maiden. I'm sure you would have been fine in a minute."

Kyra had no response to this.

"I'm Fred, by the way," he said. "I'm a traveler, exploring the countryside. This is my first time in the Kingdom of Mohr. And you must be . . ." He angled his head down at her. "Kitty?"

"Kitty?" She looked up at him, startled. She felt a pang at hearing Ariana's nickname for her in the mouth of a stranger. Get a grip, Kyra, she thought.

"It's written on your . . ." He pointed his chin toward her chest.

She felt her entire body flush as she realized he was referring to the nickname written across her soaked and clinging shift. The stitching across her left breast. She looked up sharply, but the boy's eyes were now focused straight ahead.

It was then that she realized just how naked she was: the boy's arms under her legs were touching bare skin, her shift was almost completely transparent, her belly button was in plain sight through the lace, and she didn't dare look any higher for fear of what else had become visible through the damp fabric.

Before she could actually die of embarrassment, they'd reached the shore. Kyra pushed herself out of his arms, landing on her feet in the soft sand of the riverbank.

Only to find her pig shrieking for all she was worth. The wolf had come back and was circling the large boulder.

Kyra gasped.

Fred whistled, and the wolf sat down obediently.

"Langley, I told you to stay," he said.

To the wolf.

"And I told you to sit over there." He pointed firmly to a spot ten feet away from the rock and the pig.

The wolf looked—and Kyra could barely believe this—guilty.

 50

The wolf moved to where Fred was pointing.

"He's your wolf?" Kyra asked.

Fred turned back to Kyra, a bashful smile just tweaking the corners of his mouth. "He's a dog, though I'm sure Langley takes your mistake as a compliment."

Kyra hugged her arms across her cold, soggy body and stared back at him. "He's *your* dog?"

"Um, yeah?'

"And you thought I would be *grateful* for being rescued?"

Fred's gaze dropped to his sodden traveling boots, and his hair ruffled in the breeze. Chin tilted down, he peeked up, his green-gold eyes catching her own, causing a tiny shiver to course through Kyra. He really was quite beautiful, she realized. "Maybe? A little bit?"

"But it's your fault that I fell in! If you had left when I told you to and taken your wolflike dog with you before my pig saw it, I would be dry right now. Possibly even warm."

"I sincerely apologize. I had no idea the effect Langley would have until your pig started squealing."

"Where are my clothes?" Though the sun was out, it didn't cut the chill from the river.

Then her stomach clenched. Her weapons! She hadn't been more than inches away from them in months—years, really. Even before the whole incident with the princess, she'd always had them nearby.

"I'm afraid I was only able to rescue the pig and your bag. Your clothes . . ." He shrugged.

Kyra stared hard at him. "Are you kidding me?"

His face broke into a heart-stopping smile. "Yes."

"Ugh!" Kyra resisted the urge to kick him in the shin. "You have got to be the most infuriating person I've ever met."

Gracefully, Fred reached down behind a large rock and picked up the pile of her clothes and her pack. He held out the stack and stepped back as she ripped them from his hands.

Automatically, her fingers scanned the water-slicked clothes, covertly checking that her weapons were still securely hidden in their water-repellent holsters.

"Do you mind?" She gestured for him to turn around.

His smiled turned wicked. "Don't see what difference it makes. I've already seen all there is to see."

Kyra considered pulling out a quill and putting him to sleep for a while. It wouldn't be hard. He wouldn't be expecting it, and she never missed.

Except, of course, that one time. The only time that mattered.

But missing the princess had been a statistical fluke.

One that would *not* happen again.

Kyra dismissed the thought of taking Fred out with her sleeping draft. The people hunting her would be more than a trifle interested to hear about a woman who used quills dipped in Doze.

She did have a secret up her sleeve for tough situations like this, a confusion potion that left no visible evidence, but she dismissed that idea too. The tiny swabs sewn into the sleeves of her shirt depended too much on her being unmemorable in the first place. She doubted that anything short of a full-on memory potion would make him forget the sight of a woman in absurd underclothes crossing a river with a pig on top of her head.

Kyra carefully picked her way around the rocks to a spot behind the large boulder and shook out her clothing. Water flew off, spattering the ground. She wrung out her shift, jammed her feet into the tight black pants, and immediately began to feel warmer.

She checked her pack to make sure that nothing had been broken or swept out by the current. Silt from the river had made its way in, but her gear was otherwise in order.

The pig had calmed down and was watching her curiously from its perch on the boulder.

"Let's scram," she told it.

But when she stretched her arms up, she realized she couldn't reach the pig. That annoying Fred guy must have been a good head taller than her to be able to put the pig so high up.

She couldn't just grab her pig and run.

She took a deep breath. Reaching into her bag, she removed a long polished wooden hair stick, methodically wound her wet hair up on top of her head, and pushed the stick in close to her scalp to keep the bundle in place. The deliberate, familiar movements calmed her. When she was finished, her hair was tight to her head and she felt in control again.

"Okay." She came out from behind the rock. "I need to

get my pig down, and you seem to be the only one who can reach it. Would you please get it down for me now?"

Fred smiled when he saw her. "Hey, Kitty." He greeted her like they were at a church social or something. "I would be more than happy to get your pig down for you. What's her name?" He reached down to rub a hand over his dog's head.

"My pig doesn't have a name, Fred," she said. "I'd appreciate it if you just got it down, and we'll be on our way."

He moved over to the pig. "This will just take a minute." Putting one hand firmly on the pig's rump, he held his other hand over its snout. The pig began sniffing, its face buried in the cup of his palm. "You look kind of like a Sasha to me," he said. From one of the big flap pockets of his rough green jacket, he pulled out a small dog biscuit. "Or a Rosie. Oh, Rosie's perfect."

"You CANNOT name my pig." Kyra shook her head.

"Everyone should have a name," Fred said. "Hello, little Rosie." He rubbed the pig's head as it munched contentedly on the biscuit. "You are a fine little thing. Even carry your own basket."

Kyra started as he touched the scent basket that was supposed to lead her to the princess. Miraculously, the scrap of fabric was still pinned within it. She only hoped it still worked after the dunking.

Fred stroked the pig's chin and continued to coo over her. She seemed completely oblivious to the dog sitting not ten feet away. "I'm introducing them to each other's scent," he said over his shoulder. "They'll be friends in no time."

 54

Kyra blinked hard. She had to get out of here. "They don't need to be friends."

Fred loped over to his dog and rubbed the animal's ears, his back to her. "It never hurts to have friends," he said, petting his dog with one hand, the other hand cupped around the dog's nose. He winked.

Kyra pulled the stick from her bun, and the sloppy knot of her hair came apart. She ran her thumb over the slightly thicker end of the stick, feeling the secret button that popped a tiny blade out of the other side. It was treated with a paralyzing poison. Two fast slices above a combatant's wrist would make him drop his weapon, and then a kick to the head would take him down. A few nicks . . .

No. Kyra spun away from Fred.

Across the river was the drooping willow she'd sat under earlier, back when her life had been simple. She almost laughed out loud at that—the simple life of hiding from the kingdom's soldiers and her business partners, and trying to kill her best friend.

She watched the water rush by, once again as beautiful as it had been before she'd taken an unexpected dip in it.

And then, right before Kyra's eyes, the water roiled and turned red—a deep dark red, the color of blood. The bloody river filled her vision, and the rest of the world faded away. The river stank of death.

Then she blinked and her vision was gone.

The river looked completely normal, just as it had moments before.

She hugged her black-sleeved arms around herself.

Behind her, she heard Fred talking to the animals.

"See, Rosie? Langley's a nice dog. He just wants to be friends. I know he's big and looks scary, but he's just a puppy at heart. And, Langley, you're going to have to be gentle with Rosie, okay?"

What had Fred said? He was a traveler? No job, no people to worry about, just living for the moment. What would it be like to have such an easy life?

"Here we go," he said. "Let's just set you on the ground here."

Kyra turned to find Rosie and Langley sniffing one another. They began nuzzling noses. "Hey!" Kyra shouted.

Before she could stop it, her pig was trotting off with the wolf-dog.

"You're welcome, Kitty."

Kyra caught up to the animals just as they reached what must have been Fred's camp. A small tent was set up among the trees, and a campfire was at a low smolder with a simmering pot suspended above it. She reached for the pig's leash, but it dodged away.

Fred sauntered up and pulled out another biscuit. "Here you go, Rosie."

The pig devoured the treat with relish.

"You can lunch with us if you'd like." Fred stirred the embers with a long stick, not looking at Kyra. "It's the least we can do after nearly drowning you. It's nice to have some company sometimes."

"We don't need lunch." Kyra's stomach tightened at the refusal. The campsite smelled deliciously of spices and wood smoke. Kind of like Fred himself. "We need to get going."

Fred looked up, his eyes catching Kyra's. "It was a pleasure meeting you, Kitty."

He took her hand. She pulled back, startled. "Parting gift," he said.

Kyra looked down and found a dog biscuit in her palm.

Six

ROSIE.

She couldn't believe he'd named her pig. Her worker pig. Who didn't need a name.

Kyra bit off a hunk of stale bread as she stomped through the sun-bright forest. They were on a wide birch-lined path, but Kyra saw with relief that the forest grew denser farther ahead. One problem with following a Katzenheim pig—it went down the most direct path, but it wasn't always the best route for someone who didn't want to be seen.

Fred better not have ruined Rosie's nose with all of his food and getting-the-animals-used-to-each-other business.

And the name had stuck. That's what was so infuriating. She couldn't look at the pig without thinking *Rosie*.

Fred was the most annoying kind of guy—beautiful and full of himself. He'd found the whole incident SO amusing. Kyra blushed at the memory of herself sopping wet and half naked in his arms.

Rosie kept looking up at her hopefully, as though she might have another dog biscuit in her pocket.

Kyra dropped a piece of bread for her. She ate it, but Kyra could have sworn Rosie gave her a reproachful look.

There was nothing wrong with old bread. Kyra *loved* bread. She'd pretty much been living off of it these past few months. Why did Fred have to go and tempt her with hot food and a warm fire?

What could it have been? It smelled kind of like stew, but there was a strong spicy scent of herb. It reminded her of the Gypsy food stalls at the Saturday market—sort of ethereal and woodsy, yet at the same time earthy and filling. Scrumptious. But her favorite by far was the cheese stand. They made this potato dish that was all mashed up with long strings of melty cheese whipped through it. Garlicky, buttery deliciousness.

A branch snapped behind her.

Grabbing Rosie, Kyra dove into the bushes, scratching herself on a clump of prickers. The sound had been distant but closer than it should have been. Daydreaming about food had brought her guard down.

Rosie didn't seem to mind the rough treatment. Instead of struggling, she snuggled in under Kyra's arm for a nap.

As the sound of footsteps grew closer, Kyra reached into her velvet potions bag and pulled out her cloaking charm. She spritzed herself and Rosie, and she and the pig took on the patterns of the leaves around them until their individual outlines disappeared completely.

The footsteps stopped suddenly right beside her hiding place.

Through the small spaces between the leaves, Kyra could see heavy black boots with oversized shiny silver buckles bearing the Kingdom of Mohr insignia. A king's soldier. Glancing up, all she saw was black, black, black all the way to collar height. This wasn't just any soldier; he was part of the king's special regiment. Only elite-force soldiers wore all black.

Their weapons weren't to keep the peace or disarm an opponent; they were meant to kill. Kyra knew because she had enhanced most of those weapons herself.

He thrust the tip of his sword into the hedge and leaned forward to look inside. She had to stop herself from gasping as she recognized the man's chin-length black hair framing a drooping mustache. Dartagn.

Of all the soldiers to be after her.

He had *trained* her.

Dartagn crouched down and peered deeper into the bushes. The tip of his sword, glowing green with poison, was inches away.

Behind him came the *ffffeeet, ffffeeet, ffffeeet* of a small animal scurrying toward them. Dartagn paused to listen.

The animal stopped a few feet away. A squirrel.

Kyra held her breath.

Please leave, please leave, please leave.

She felt Dartagn hesitate.

Kyra palmed a small rock and flicked it to land a scant inch from the squirrel's tail. The animal took off, shooting out from beneath the pricker bush onto the path in front of Dartagn.

He swore to himself and stood up. His black boots moved away.

Kyra slowly let out a deep breath, but stayed where she was. Once she was sure there was absolutely no chance that Dartagn was still in the area, she stood. She shook the invisible pig in her arms and heard her wake with a loud yawn.

Kyra held tight to her end of the leash as she deposited Rosie on the ground. "So glad you got a nice nap in."

Kyra spent the rest of the day following Rosie and alternately jumping at every sound that might be Dartagn or another elite-force soldier.

And obsessing about food.

The memory of that spicy stew of Fred's haunted her. How could someone so annoying make something that smelled so good?

The sun was sinking into the horizon when Kyra heard noises behind her that could only be footsteps.

She dove into the bushes with Rosie for the second time that day and waited for whoever it was to pass by.

Just as the footsteps drew near, Kyra looked again at the pig and realized that she was as solid and pink as could be. The cloaking charm had faded. How had she let that happen?

The footsteps and shuffling noises grew closer.

And closer.

She didn't want to risk the noise of her cloaking mister.

The next thing Kyra knew, a wet nose was thrust into her face.

And a tongue licked her.

A dog's tongue.

"Come on, Langley," Fred's voice called, already walking away. "There's nothing in there."

What was *he* doing here?

Kyra held her breath.

Langley pulled his head out of the bushes, and Kyra heard him shuffling off after Fred.

A few moments later she heard a loud shout, followed by a scream.

Seven

KYRA RAN DOWN THE path and came to the top of a rise just in time to see a goblin smash Fred in the head with a club.

Fred fell to the ground.

Langley growled low in his throat and placed himself between the goblin and Fred.

There were six goblins in all—vicious, gray-skinned creatures with oversized globelike eyes, sharp teeth, and knotted muscles. They were shorter than an average man—just about Kyra's size. The one with the club circled around the big dog as another goblin with a long wicked knife advanced head-on, one eye on Langley, one eye on Fred's pack. The others crowded around and snickered.

Goblins were the worst. It wouldn't be enough to steal the

unconscious man's bag. They'd slit his throat, and Langley's, too—and then probably make a meal of them both before leaving.

She had to do something. But what? Goblins didn't react to potions the same way that humans did. There was something different in their body chemistry that skewed the effects of potions, often with surprising and horrible results.

She was going to have to do this the old-fashioned way.

"Stay here," she whispered to Rosie. She grabbed a couple of egg-sized rocks.

Kyra whipped one of the rocks at the goblin on the far left. It hit his skull with a loud crack, and he collapsed, stunned. She nailed a second with another rock, dropping him too.

Now there were only four.

With an enormous leap, Kyra landed beside Fred and the growling dog. Right in front of the goblin with the knife.

She slammed the side of her hand against his wrist, and his weapon flew to the ground. A quick jab to his throat and a sweep of her leg, and he was down just in time for her to jam her elbow into the solar plexus of a goblin who'd come at her from behind.

Another swiped at her with one long-nailed hand.

In the quick, measured moves she'd been taught by Dartagn, she locked the goblin's arm, kicked him in the stomach, and sent him sprawling. She turned on the goblin with the club just as a shadow fell on them both.

A dark, winged creature flew up above the fray.

A greck.

It came at Kyra, a foul-smelling leathery wing brushing her face as it alighted on her head. Pinpoint claws scrabbled against her scalp, reaching for her eyes. Grecks, she knew, blinded their prey and then used their long pointed beaks to crack open their victim's skull.

As she reached up to tear the greck from her head, the goblin with the club ran at her, and the greck's talons sank in just above her eyebrows.

Kyra rolled to the side and kicked her leg straight up, smacking the goblin in the jaw. He fell back, and she grabbed the club, swinging it up at her own head. It connected with the greck with a satisfying squelch. The thing shrilled and loosened its grip.

It took two more swings until the greck released her and slid off her head.

Kyra wiped the blood from her eyes and glared at the three goblins that were back on their feet. "Come on," she said, waving the club.

Shrieking, one leaped at her and she batted it aside. It tumbled to the ground and lay unmoving.

The remaining two looked at each other and then sprinted away, leaving their companions. For one second, the club raised over her head, Kyra almost chased after them.

She stopped herself.

There was no real danger that they would spread tales about the human girl who beat them—no one listened to goblins.

Except Arlo.

There had been goblins at Arlo's. Had he sent these to ambush her? But why would he do that? For once, Kyra's goal and Arlo's were the same.

As long as she'd known of him, Arlo had been plotting to destroy the kingdom. When Kyra was little, he'd even managed to get bear trolls into the palace. They'd killed three people before the guards managed to contain them. And he was rumored to be behind even worse attempts on the royals.

But Arlo never got punished for his crimes against the kingdom because no one could ever prove he was responsible. He always got someone else to do his dirty deeds. Someone else to take the blame while he walked free.

Someone like Kyra.

Kyra tore a strip of cloth from the hem of her shirt. She wiped the blood off her face and tentatively touched the holes the greck's claws had made. They stung, but she could tell the wounds weren't deep. She couldn't quite shake the sensation of it up there, feeling like it was about to suck her life away.

Kyra tied the cloth around her forehead to stanch the blood.

She had to get Fred out of there before the goblins regained consciousness.

Lowering herself to her knees, Kyra pulled Fred and his pack across her shoulders. Carefully, she stood up.

"Oof," she said. Fred was not a small person. He was at least a head taller than she was, and a good half a person wider.

She caught Rosie watching her from the top of the hill. At least she'd stayed put. "Come on, Rosie. Langley."

The animals fell in line behind her as she staggered out of the clearing and into the forest, putting as much distance between themselves and the goblins as possible.

A half hour later, when she could carry him no farther and hoped they were a safe distance, Kyra collapsed and dropped Fred to the ground. She shrugged off his pack and her own, and propped him up against a tree. For a pretty young man, he sure weighed a lot.

"Fred," she wheezed. "Wake up."

He had to regain consciousness soon. She couldn't carry him any farther, and she didn't have any healing potions.

She sat back on her heels, considering. There was water in her canteen. She could at least try to clean his wound.

Before she could do that, Langley began licking Fred's face.

His striking green-gold eyes fluttered open. "Kitty?"

"Hello, Fred." Kyra set down her canteen.

"What happened? The last thing I remember was a pack of goblins coming at me." He reached up to touch his head, winced, and came away with blood on his fingertips. "Ouch."

"I think the goblins hit you on the head." She sat back on her heels and thought quickly. "By the time I got there, they'd been chased away."

"By what?" He blinked beautifully. "Do you know you have blood all down your face? You look awful."

"Gee, thanks." She wet a corner of her shirt and scrubbed at her face. One of the tricks to lying was to keep the story close to the truth. "A pack of grecks went after the goblins, but one got me before he took off after the rest."

That sounded more believable than that she'd single-handedly taken on a pack of goblins and a greck.

"So you tried to save me." Fred's smile lit up his face.

"I thought they were all gone when I found you. Don't get any ideas."

"But you must have moved me."

"Just in case they came back."

"So you tried to save me." He just kept smiling at her.

"You're insufferable. How can you keep smiling with that giant gash on your head?"

He reached for his pack and pulled out a small jar. "Very special super healing balm," he said as he unscrewed the lid. "It takes the sting out of any scrape or cut without so much as a whisper of a scar left behind."

Fred dabbed some onto his head wound, wincing with every tap.

He handed the jar to Kyra.

It smelled like sunshine. Kyra unwound the strip of cloth around her head and patted the mixture lightly on her own injuries. She tried to conjure up pages from her medical potions textbook to pinpoint what had gone into the mixture, but the only image that came to mind was her crabby medical potions instructor glaring at her as he pulled out a copy of *Effective Coatings for Blade Metals and Alloys* from where she'd been covertly reading it behind her textbook.

"Can you walk?" Kyra said, taking the bandage Fred handed her. "We should keep moving. We're not that far away from where they attacked you."

He smoothed a bandage on his own head and stood up slowly. "Yeah, I think so." He wobbled a little bit. "Whoa."

Kyra stepped beside him and let him put his arm around her shoulder. They started walking, Fred leaning on her. "You'd better not be faking."

Fred chuckled. "So, how did you happen to be so close by?"

"I was going to ask you the same question."

"Langley. He was following a trail, pulling me along all day. I assumed he was hunting a rabbit or something." Fred looked down and started shaking with laughter. "I'm so stupid."

She followed his gaze and saw Rosie and Langley avidly sniffing each other. "You have got to be kidding me."

"Love," Fred said. "It does the strangest things to you, doesn't it?" He reached down and vigorously rubbed the dog's head. "I had no idea you were such a romantic, Langley."

When he stood again, he seemed steadier on his feet. "Good thing we caught some fish before we set out, as that elusive rabbit seems to have turned into a figment of my imagination."

Fresh fish. Kyra's stomach growled. It was like the clouds had parted and delivered her greatest wish. She was probably drooling. There was his fishing rod poking straight up out of the top of his pack. "I didn't think to bring my reel on this trip," she said.

"I wouldn't leave home without it. Towns are few and far between in this part of the world. Makes it difficult to stock up on supplies without grubbing for some of it yourself. And there's nothing like fresh fish."

"I wasn't really thinking about that when I left home."

"Your trip probably isn't quite as extended as mine."

"Why would you say that?" Kyra realized she was revealing too much. Damn her hungry belly.

But Fred just shrugged. "You don't exactly look equipped for a long journey."

Little did he know it had already lasted three months. "Yeah, um, that's true. It's just a short trip to my sis— I mean, cousin's house. Delivering the pig, you know, as a gift. To her. Well, really, his kid. I mean, her kid. Right. So anyway, it's only a few days' journey and I didn't plan that well."

She had spoken to so few people in the past three months that she didn't really have much practice lying.

"You're giving Rosie away?" Fred's green-gold eyes watched the small pig in front of him. "To be a kid's pet?"

"Yup."

"I never would have guessed it. She seems so attached to you. Sort of sophisticated for a kid's pet, too."

"Sophisticated?"

"Yes, sophisticated. Don't give me that look. She has a very distinct personality, and it's most certainly not the rough-and-tumble-with-kids kind."

"We'll see."

"Yes, you will." Fred squeezed her arm gently.

The long shadows of sunset had disappeared and dusk was settling when Kyra heard water tumbling over rocks up ahead. As they broke through the trees, the *shush-shush*ing of the water grew louder. There was a stream, no more than a sword's length across, falling over a small rocky ledge to a clear pool below.

"Perfect," Kyra said, thinking immediately of her laundry.

"For?"

"We should make camp soon, don't you think?" Kyra asked.

"So I'm going to have the pleasure of your company this evening? I had the idea that you were against socializing with strange men."

"It's going to be full-on night soon. It just makes sense to share camp tonight." Then she realized that a young man like Fred, especially a young man who looked the way Fred did, could take that invitation *entirely* wrong. "I mean—you know—in a friendly sort of way."

His eyes crinkled at the corners in amusement. "As opposed to an unfriendly sort of way."

"Er, yes."

"Sure." Fred ran his hands through his perpetually rumpled brown hair, seeming to forget his wound, and flinching. "I suppose we could do that."

"Well, you don't have to sound so excited about it."

"I would be honored to share a fire with you, Kitty. In a friendly sort of way."

Eight

FRED STARTED BUILDING a fire from bits of leaves and twigs in a small clearing. "We're going to need more wood."

"I'll get it!" Kyra said. "I have some, uh, other things to attend to anyway." No way was she wearing these undergarments one more day when there was a perfectly good stream to do laundry in just down the hill. "I'll get the wood on my way back."

"*Things* to attend to?" Fred looked up, small puffs of smoke rising in front of his face.

"I have some items of clothing I need to clean. Which I'm going to go do. Down at the stream. By myself."

"Didn't everything you own get soaked when you took a dive into the river earlier?"

"Getting something wet doesn't make it clean. You don't do laundry by dipping it in water and hoping for the best."

"You don't?"

Kyra grabbed her pack and set off down the hill.

"You need some help?" He called after her. "I'm really good at dipping things in water and hoping for the best."

"I'll be just fine, thank you."

Fred shrugged and put another twig on the fire.

At the stream, Kyra squirted her Rapid Cleaning potion onto her dirty clothes—and her more *practical* underthings, simply cut shifts and bottoms made with plain soft cloth. No bows, see-through sections, or embroidered cats. A fine layer of silt from the Iota River had made its way into everything. Gently, Kyra swished the clothes in the water, watching the sediment float off into the clear current.

Swish, swish, swish.

What was she doing camping with a handsome stranger when she should be out hunting down the princess?

Well, she had to eat and sleep, didn't she? She'd fought goblins, after all. And a greck! And it really would be irresponsible to leave Fred alone so soon after his head injury. Just one night of good food and a warm fire. That wouldn't be so bad, would it?

Kyra wrung out her clothes and went back up the hill. She stopped just short of their campsite and delicately hung each item out to dry on the branches of a couple of tiny pines.

"Kyra?" Fred's voice came through the trees. "Is that you?"

"Just getting firewood, be right there."

Several armfuls of wood and degrees of darkness later, Kyra sat across the fire from Fred, slicing potatoes with a camp knife.

Fred, the sleeves of his jacket rolled up, drizzled oil on the trout fillets and sprinkled them with seasoning he'd pulled from his pack. Rosie and Langley were sleeping together under a tree—the big dog curled around the tiny pig, the pig's muzzle tucked into the dog's belly.

The sun was completely gone, leaving only bare pink streaks in the sky. Dark outlines of trees surrounded their camp, and at the center was the crackling fire. Kyra never dared to have a fire—it would attract too much attention—but she felt safe having one with Fred. No one was on the lookout for *two* travelers—just for one decidedly unfriendly woman.

The potatoes were sprinkled with fresh herbs and placed into Fred's small round cooking pot, which Kyra covered and placed carefully in the center of the coals.

While Fred wrapped the fish in a cooking packet, Kyra picked up his seasoning jar and tried to read the words written on the label by the light of her necklace.

"You won't be able to read it," Fred said, without glancing at her. "It's written in Cryptic Lorienne."

"And you can read Cryptic Lorienne?"

Fred laid the fish packet beside the pot. "I've picked up a thing or two in my travels, though I've never seen anything quite like that necklace. Where did you get it?"

Kyra cupped her hands around the glowing stone. "A friend."

"Thoughtful friend to give you something both beautiful and useful."

"I guess so."

"It suits you."

"That almost sounds like a compliment."

"I think you've underestimated what a nice guy I am. Compliments and dinner—really, Kitty, what woman could resist?"

"Save the compliments. I'm here for the food."

Kyra smiled to herself and watched the glowing coals.

"What?" she asked when she realized Fred was watching her from the other side of the fire, the light flickering across his face.

"Nothing." He shook his head. "You seem unusually relaxed."

"You've pretty much only seen me drowning and running from goblins, so you haven't got all that much to go on."

"True. But you really seem to enjoy"—he spread his hands wide—"thinking about dinner."

"Yeah, well, one of my roommates said it was either incredibly freaky genetics or a gift from the gods that I'm not enormously fat. I like food. I like mixing ingredients and discovering how they work together." Tiny little flames reached around the coals to lick the potato pot.

"You sound like my dad talking about work. He's always going on about the essential qualities of different perfumes and how they combine."

"Really?" The charcoaley smell of roasted fish and vegetables was starting to scent the air between them, and the warm glow of the fire had heated Kyra straight through. She felt strangely safe in the patch of firelight inside the dense surrounding of trees.

Fred shrugged. "Family business. Unfortunately, as the youngest son, there wasn't much room for me, so I decided to take off and travel, see what the world has to offer."

"I can't imagine. I've always known exactly what I wanted to do."

"What is that?"

Kyra's muscles tensed. "Um . . . dairymaid."

"You're a dairymaid?"

"Yep."

"Huh. So, what, you like, make butter and stuff?"

Dairymaid? Couldn't she have come up with something better than that? She guessed it could be worse—she did have more than a passing knowledge of dairy craft. Domestic Studies were a required part of potioner training. Of course, she'd grumbled like all of the other apprentices, but her Hiccoughing Butter and Sweet Dreams Pots de Crème had gotten top scores. Honestly, she loved potions almost no matter what area they were in. Even cosmetics came in handy—she'd learned how to make a glamour that changed her appearance when she needed a disguise.

"Mm-hm," Kyra said, in answer to Fred's question. "So tell me about this olive oil. Where's it from?"

She relaxed again as the subject switched back to cooking. She didn't know why she was feeling so comfortable. Somewhere deep in her bones she knew it was dangerous to feel that way.

Her first bite of fish made the niggling feeling of danger evaporate immediately. "This is *so* good. What is in that spice mix?"

"Now, I may be a lot of things, Kitty, but a spoiler of ancient Lorienne secret recipes I am not. You'll have to learn the language and find out."

Kyra threw a pinecone at him. Then took a bite of potatoes.

Fred chuckled, catching the expression on Kyra's face.

"What?" she said, her mouth full. "It's really good!"

He nodded, still watching her. "I'm glad you're enjoying it so much." He reached out and added wood to the campfire before turning to his own meal.

The conversation fell away as they dug into their food.

The flames grew, crackling as they licked the fresh tinder. The fire shifted and sparks flew up into the air between them.

Kyra ate slowly, savoring each tasty forkful.

When the last bit of fish and potatoes were gone, Fred leaned back on his elbows across the fire. "So, you've got roommates?"

Kyra answered with care. "Two of them. They're my business partners—we have a dairy business together."

"It seems like that would be a lot of time together, living and working with the same people."

"Usually we get along just fine. Sometimes better than others. But we all love what we're doing." This was completely true, and it wrenched Kyra for a moment. She was the one who'd brought them together to form the Master Trio—she'd seen in Hal's and Ned's eyes the same passion for potionery and had known they would make an amazing team. They were both a few years older, and Kyra had attended lectures by them while still an apprentice.

Hal's lectures had drawn huge crowds—mostly giggling girls, many of whom weren't even potioners. Kyra didn't care that he was handsome—in fact, his fussy blue silk and velvet outfit might have turned her away if not for the spark in his eyes when he presented his ideas. His potion theories were revolutionary, and he seemed to have a passion for his work.

When Kyra finally extended an invitation to join her in business, she wrote him the most formal letter possible. She wanted him to know right from the start how serious she was.

Ned's lecture, on the other hand, had been poorly attended despite the name he'd made for himself, but he hadn't seemed to mind. His clothes fell in wrinkles over his big belly, and it looked like he'd just randomly picked them up off the floor; but when he spoke he'd had the same spark as Hal.

Ned had ended his lecture by saying, "So, yeah, that's what I'm working on right now, but, hey, you don't want to hear me yammer on anymore. Anyone up for some meat loaf? I've heard the place across the street has the best."

Kyra had gone with him, but only because she felt bad.

She felt worse after tasting the meat loaf. "Actually," she said, "I'm pretty sure mine's better."

Ned's round face lit up. "Do you use cumin? I don't know why more people don't use it. It's pricey, but a small investment for so much goodness."

Later, when she'd written to invite *him* to join the business, she'd included a recipe for her most recent improvement to meat loaf.

In the end, though, she hadn't chosen them for their personalities or how they dressed. She'd chosen them because they were the best at what they did, and because they both loved potions. Just like she did.

When things had been good, energy sparked through the flat, and they made potions and poisons that did things no one would have ever thought possible. Everything seemed right with the world. The memories caused Kyra to ache all over, knowing these events would never happen again.

She realized that Fred was watching her. His eyes flickered with the flames from the fire. She looked away.

"You really *do* love your work, don't you?" Fred said. "I can see it on your face when you're thinking about it."

"Yeah, I guess I do."

"I've never felt anything like that. Watching you makes me feel like I'm missing out on something."

Kyra couldn't meet his eyes. "It isn't so easy. There's always a price for love."

Fred was quiet for a minute, and he came around the fire to her side. His shoulder brushed against hers. "I don't know anything about working, but I do know a little something about love."

Kyra's breath caught in her throat, but when she looked up she saw he was smiling, his face inches away from her own.

"Have you ever heard the song 'My Love's a Bonny Lady, if Only She Weren't a Fish'?"

"Is it about a mermaid?"

Fred shook his head. "Nope."

Fred taught her the song, and soon she was joining in on the refrain:

Her skin's as pretty as lilies, her eyes as bright as a star,

If only she could come up here, she'd be the prettiest girl by far.

Alas, she's under the ocean, I cannot kiss her there,

For whenever I duck my head under, I come gasping up for air.

A kiss, a kiss, I'd give my fish a kiss.

My lady lies under the ocean where I cannot get a kiss.

Fred beamed at her as she finished the verse. "Okay," he said, "now you've got to learn the hand motions. Keep rhythm with your foot and lift your hand up as though you've got a mug of beer in it."

He raised her arm and folded her fingers around an imaginary mug handle. "Now pretend you're in the pub, swinging the mug to the tune, and when you get to the part 'whenever I duck my head under,' duck your head"—gently, he pushed her head down and to the side—"and tip the mug. It's not quite as entertaining without the beer actually splashing down on your face, but you get the idea."

Kyra's long hair caressed her cheek. From that angle she asked, "Are you serious? You pour beer on your face?"

"Well, you aim for your mouth."

"I'm sure this is extremely popular with pub owners."

"If it keeps the customers happy . . . Once through with the hand motions?"

For some reason, the ridiculous drinking song reminded Kyra of her dad. He would love Fred.

Kyra quashed the thought as quickly as it had sprung up on her. She couldn't think of her family.

They sang it through together, complete with imaginary beer. The way he watched her sing made her feel as undressed as she'd been when they'd first met.

When they finished, Fred picked up the cooking pot. "I'm going to go give this a quick rinse."

Kyra was warm all over. She pulled her bedroll out and snuggled down into it.

A few minutes later, a chuckle came from behind her. "Kitty, don't be alarmed, but this part of the forest seems to be populated by a bush I've never seen before."

"Hmmm . . . ?"

"It seems to be sprouting women's underthings."

Kyra sat bolt upright. "Leave those underthings alone."

Fred sat beside her. "I wouldn't dream of touching such an unusual plant. It's probably poisonous."

"Ha-ha."

"Well, it isn't as though I haven't seen them before. Though I must say, I think I'm more fond of that lacy see-through model I saw you in earlier."

"Good night, Fred." Kyra lay back down on her bedroll.

"'Night, Kitty."

Kyra smiled despite herself. She shut her eyes and, feeling fed and content for the first time in a long time, fell right to sleep.

Kyra woke before dawn the next morning with a start, cold wet dew clinging to her meager blanket. Rosie had sought her out sometime in the night and was curled beside her under the damp cover. Fred was less than a foot away in his own bedroll, sleeping as though he hadn't a care in the world. For one second she wanted to curl back up and sink into the warm feeling she'd fallen asleep with.

What was she doing? Kyra sat up, shivering.

Last night there had been *singing*.

She had been singing.

And the way Fred had looked at her when they were singing . . .

She'd acted like some crazy pleasure-potion addict last night. Practically selling her soul for a single hot-cooked meal. She was the potions weapons expert, a dangerous assassin living on the fringes of society. She was tracking the princess. In order to *kill* her. People like her did not share friendly campfires with strange young men. Especially not young men like Fred.

No, she consorted with criminals. Kyra felt suddenly sick all over again at the thought of working with Arlo.

She needed to focus on her mission.

Fred was still sleeping, his face completely relaxed.

She carefully moved the sleeping pig to one side, rose, and quietly rolled up her bedding and blanket. She tied it to her pack, then silently left a stack of coins by the fire, where she knew Fred would find them.

Scribbling "Thanks" with a stick in the dirt, Kyra hesitated, then signed "Kitty" after it.

She tucked the pig under her arm, plucked her underthings from the trees, and set off on her own.

Once she was far enough away from the campsite, she set the little pig on the ground, and Rosie dutifully snuffled and led the way forward. Every now and then, she turned her little pink face back to make sure Kyra was behind her.

Kyra wanted to shout, "Of course I'm following you! You're the seeking pig!"

But she didn't. It wasn't Rosie's fault Kyra was in such a bad mood.

Nine

"ARE YOU SURE THIS is the right way, Rosie? Absolutely sure?"

Rosie grunted good-naturedly and kept going. So much for solidarity.

"Because you seem to be taking us toward Wexford, and I'd really rather go pretty much anywhere else but there."

Wexford. The capital city with the beautiful and impregnable palace on the hill. Where Kyra had served the princess. And from which Kyra had moved away as soon as she'd graduated from her apprenticeship—both to start the Master Trio and to get away from the prying eyes of people like the Duchess Genria. And to which Kyra had returned in order to kill the princess.

The sun had only just cleared the tops of the trees when Kyra heard the long-legged lope and shuffling sound that could only be one person. And his dog.

She should have walked faster.

Kyra waited until they turned up on the path. "Why are you following me?"

"And I would want to follow you because . . . ?" Fred's lips were tight and one eyebrow was arched. "I wanted to hang out in a 'friendly sort of way'? To get ditched again? Hmmm . . . No, I don't think so." His cheeks were flushed with anger. "You know, Kitty, it may not have occurred to you, but there are plenty of women who'd enjoy spending time with me. I appreciate your saving my life and all—"

"I didn't—"

"Of course you didn't." He folded his arms across his chest. "Why would you save someone you wouldn't even bother saying good-bye to?"

Kyra shrugged and looked at her feet.

"As it happens, Langley and I are going to Wexford for supplies. It seems as though you're heading in the same direction."

For a second, there seemed to be genuine hurt in his eyes. Then it disappeared and he reached into one of his jacket pockets.

"And this . . ." Fred picked up her hand and turned it palm up. One by one, he dropped her coins into it. The coins made a steady *cling, cling, cling* as they fell. "I don't even know where to start. You don't know the first thing about people or friendship." He held her hand for a moment, staring her down with his green-gold eyes. "Believe me, I'm not following you."

And then he left her there.

Tears—something she hadn't experienced in a long time—pricked her eyes. How had she'd managed to smash the good nature out of the happiest person she'd ever met?

Suddenly Kyra was running after him. "Fred!"

Rosie kept pace, and they both skidded to a halt when they caught up to him. "I'm sorry. I've been a jerk. Can we start over?"

"Why?"

"Because . . ." Kyra realized she had little to nothing to recommend herself. "I know a great song about a man who falls in love with a songbird?"

"Really?"

"No."

Fred ducked his head, but Kyra thought she saw the ghost of a grin, and he didn't move away when she started walking by his side.

"But I do know some dirty jokes," she said. She had no idea why she wanted him to like her. It was insane. She had more important things to worry about. But she never wanted him to look at her again the way he had earlier. It made her . . . uncomfortable.

Gods, was she really that lonely?

It wasn't just Fred's stunning features, or the tight muscles across his stomach she glimpsed when his shirt rode up. She knew better than to get mixed up with good-looking men, and Fred was undeniably that. But he was so much more. When he wasn't being completely infuriating (and sometimes even when he was), he radiated joy like a beam of light. She caught just a tiny bit of that warmth when she was with him.

She wasn't sure she deserved to feel that warmth. But she craved it all the same.

"Well, then," he said, smiling again, "I suppose you can keep us company a while longer. Langley likes dirty jokes, don't you, boy?"

And just like that she was forgiven.

They walked, and Kyra tried to suppress the knowledge that she would have to abandon Fred again. Sometime very soon. As soon as he met anyone else in the kingdom, he'd hear about the Princess Killer. She hoped somehow that he wouldn't make the connection to her.

"Okay, that one's pretty good," Fred acknowledged, after she'd told him a particularly filthy joke. "But have you heard the one about the baker's wife?"

"No," Kyra said.

"Rumor has it, she married him for his buns." Fred burst out laughing.

Kyra groaned. "Okay, that was just bad."

Up ahead, Rosie was happily snuffling along the forest floor, pausing every now and then to make moony eyes at Langley. Kyra might have been suspicious of the pig's duty to the job at hand, but Rosie's nose was still at work between glances at the big dog.

"So," Kyra said, trying to sound casual, "does your dad work with potioners in his perfume business?"

Fred shook his head. "Where I come from, perfume is strictly to make things smell nice. The Perfumers Guild doesn't allow any potioners."

"What business is it of the guild's? Why do they care?"

"That's just the rule."

"That's exactly what's wrong with guilds. They think they can control everything. I don't know how it is where you come from, but here the king isn't just head of the army, he's also the head of all the guilds. If he doesn't like something, then he bans it for everyone. But the king isn't trained in everything, so how can he know what's best?"

"Whoa," Fred said, glancing around nervously, "you might want to keep the anti-royalist sentiment down. People can lose their heads for criticizing the king."

"I'm not criticizing the king. I was just commenting on the guilds. They really just want to control everything you produce and bully everyone. I would *never* join the guild!"

"Dairymaids have a guild?" Fred was looking at her curiously.

Kyra opened her mouth to argue that *of course* there was a Dairymaid Guild, even though really she had no idea, but realized that she couldn't move.

She was frozen in her tracks, her mouth stuck open with her retort.

And by the unusual silence coming from Fred's direction, he must have been, too.

A cackling laugh came from behind them.

"What do we have here?" an old lady said in a rubbing-her-hands-together-with-glee tone of voice. "Never know what my sticky traps are going to bring me."

A witch.

It had to be. The freeze wasn't any kind of potion magic that Kyra knew.

Kyra really, really didn't like witches.

The witch moved closer, her footsteps slow.

"Now, this one is really quite handsome," the old lady said. "I'm going to free up your legs, and you're going to follow me. I wouldn't suggest making a run for it." She chortled. "Or *do*—it's always such fun to have a challenge."

A sound of footsteps walking away. Kyra had the urge to shudder, but the spell kept her frozen in place. It was like she had a solid wood veneer over the surface of her skin.

At least she was still breathing. A breeze pushed Kyra's hair across her face and into her eyes. Mosquitoes buzzed by her ears. She felt them land on her and bite.

What was taking so long?

She could feel Rosie's leash in her hand but couldn't see her. She hoped the pig wasn't panicking. Yes, she was just a pig, but Kyra figured it had to be scary to not understand why suddenly you couldn't move.

When Kyra thought she couldn't stand it for one more minute, she heard the puttering footsteps come back. An extremely old woman with the look of an ancient bird of prey came into view and yanked the leash out of her frozen fingers. Then she reached down to pick up Rosie.

"The same goes for you. I'll free your legs, but only so you can follow me."

A pressure disappeared on Kyra's lower half.

"This way."

Kyra followed, considering her options. She had no idea how to unfreeze her upper body. She didn't know that much about witches' magic—only that it was bound up with the witch's will. Possibly the witch would either have to lose interest or die before the spell would evaporate.

They approached an old tumbledown cottage, weeds growing up all around it and multicolored glass baubles spinning from the trees. It smelled like . . . herbs, fresh-picked, but with an undertone of something else, something powerful and scary.

She spied Fred as the witch led her into the small dark house. He was sitting at a rough-hewn table, a kitchen fire behind him casting him in silhouette. As Kyra drew closer, the dim light from the one small kitchen window revealed that Fred's face was stuck in a skeptical reaction to what she had been saying.

The witch pushed down on Kyra's shoulders until she was seated just around the table from Fred. "I have need of workers . . . but first we'll have to run some tests."

She set a battered leather toolbox on the table. Opening the lid, the witch pulled out a long thin piece of metal with a wicked-looking point, which she proceeded to poke into each of their index fingers. She scooped the bubbles of blood onto a small glass tray and studied them.

"Healthy, anyway."

This was ridiculous. *Just unfreeze us so we can kick your butt and go*, Kyra thought. There was no future in which Kyra was going to be this woman's slave.

Another silver instrument appeared in the witch's hands, this one a glass tube with a colored bead inside, which changed hue as she tapped Fred's and Kyra's temples with it. She grunted. "Troublemakers, though.

"And finally . . ." Out came a flat glass disk.

Kyra's stomach would have clenched if she'd had control over that part of her body. She knew what this was, and she sincerely wished she were anywhere but here.

She watched the witch peer through the disk somewhere in the direction of Fred's midsection. "Completely clean. Still, you might do as a woodcutter or something. And you *are* awfully nice to look at." Her smile sent a chill through the unfrozen parts of Kyra.

Then it was Kyra's turn. The witch squinted at Kyra's midsection. "Well . . . what a nice surprise: a spark."

The woman's beaky nose thrust into Kyra's face, her penetrating gray eyes staring into Kyra's own. "You've got the witch's spark . . . but you haven't kindled it at all. Tried to stomp it out, more like. Used your magic, what, once? Twice, maybe? Why would you ignore a gift like that?"

Abruptly, Kyra was freed from the neck up. Her open mouth closed, and she squinted her eyes shut as hard as she could. If only she could open them and find something other than a nasty old witch.

No such luck.

"I'm waiting for an answer." The witch was only inches away.

"I'm not going to become a witch."

"Witches are born, not made. And it's too late for you. You are what you are."

Kyra winced. She was NOT a witch. She'd never asked to be born with the stupid spark of witchcraft inside her, and she'd never encouraged it. The few times her gift had unwillingly come to her had been complete and total disasters. Kyra was a *potioner*—practitioner of a *logical* science, one with rules and structure. When you followed the recipe, things turned out right.

"Are you going to tell me what your specialty is, or am I going to have to force it out of you?" The witch eyed her grimly.

"Generalist." No way was Kyra going to tell this witch that she had the Sight.

"Oh, I don't believe that. Generalists don't get scared off and ignore their gifts."

Kyra would have shrugged if she could, but all she could move was her head. She turned and saw that Rosie and Langley were unfrozen, but sat huddled and terrified near the door.

Why don't I start with slicing off this boy's ear here?" The witch looked at Fred. "He certainly doesn't need both of them to take orders from me."

She picked a knife out of her toolbox.

"I'm a Seer," Kyra said quickly; and added a lie. "But I've only had one vision."

"Such a useful skill!" The witch lowered her knife. "Why hide from it?"

Kyra looked back defiantly, saying nothing. She'd been five years old when she'd had her first vision: a murdered woman and child being set on fire in their kitchen. Horrifying. Even at five she'd known it was a true vision, and knew there was no way she could help them.

"You could do so much." The witch narrowed her eyes. "*Will* do so much now that you belong to me. Though"—she raised the glass disk again, her eyes boring into Kyra—"you've been touched by an obeeka."

"I don't know what that is."

"You wouldn't. Obeekas are extremely rare." The old crone pursed her lips. "Anyone or anything around you make you feel *unsettled* lately? Weak, clumsy, or dimmer than usual?"

Kyra couldn't help but think of Fred. Supernatural powers would explain a lot about why she was so flustered around him. Then she thought back further to Arlo and his creepy black-eyed minions. And further back still to the vision that had set her on this path: a creative lording over a destroyed kingdom. "*Everything* has me unsettled lately," she answered at last.

"No matter," the witch said. "If there's an obeeka after you, we'll deal with it when the time comes. Now, let's get the matter of ownership settled and make your slave status official."

The witch pointed at Fred and said a small charm. "You, go get me a piece of paper and a quill from my writing desk."

Fred mechanically rose and fetched the paper and pen.

The witch took both, sat beside Kyra, and started writing up a document. Sweat trickled down Kyra's back.

Over the old woman's shoulder, Kyra glared at Fred. He shrugged and raised his eyebrows.

Kyra carefully mouthed, stressing each syllable, *Do. Some. Thing.*

Fred looked at a complete loss. He mouthed back, *Like what?* and put his hands up questioningly.

Hit. Her. Kyra nodded her head forcefully at the witch's head, in case he didn't get it.

The witch looked up, directly at Kyra. "Having a twitch, dear?"

"Stiff neck."

"That'll happen with a freeze spell. Speaking of which . . ." She pointed over her shoulder at Fred and muttered, and his body immediately refroze, leaving only his face mobile.

The witch went back to work.

Kyra rolled her eyes in frustration.

The old woman leaned back. "Done! Now, you just need to put your mark here and we'll be all set. I'm going to release you so you can use your hands." She spoke the words to undo the spell, and Kyra prepared to slap the poison cells on her pants.

But before she could act, Fred said, "You can't bind her."

"Oh, I most certainly can. That's what we do here, dear. I'll be doing you next."

"We're married."

"What?" The witch hissed and spat on the floor.

Kyra had to admit, it was a smart move on Fred's part.

Marriages involved complicated magic so that the groom and bride belonged not only to each other but to the land as well. There was no more powerful spell than a Nuptial Bond.

"A fully binding marriage agreement?" The look of shock on the witch's face was replaced by suspicion. "Neither of you wear rings."

"We were too poor," Kyra said. "I got this." She pulled out her necklace. It glowed in the dim light of the cottage.

"And I got a pocket watch." Fred looked at the witch hopefully, and when she released him, he pulled a shiny pocket watch out of his pants. "To remind me to come home to dinner on time," he said, grinning.

Only Fred would feel that now was the time to joke. Kyra prayed the witch would let them go and they wouldn't have to fight her. She was a bit too quick with the spell-casting for Kyra's liking.

"Was your Nuptial Bond created by a registered witch?" the old woman asked.

"The witchiest," Fred said.

The witch was breathing hard now. *"Married."* She looked like she was going to explode. "I don't *do* married." The witch thrust out her hand. "Give them to me." When they didn't move fast enough, she muttered a spell. "The necklace and the watch. Now!"

Kyra's hand moved of its own accord and dropped the necklace into the witch's palm, right atop Fred's watch. The witch shoved them into the outer pocket of her patchwork dress as she muttered angrily, "Ridiculous marriage binding charms, keeping an honest witch from her work, stupid fertility witches, think they know everything, most worthless career I ever heard . . ."

Kyra and Fred edged toward the door.

"We should probably get going," Fred said. "We wouldn't want to keep you from your busy schedule; no doubt you've got newts to skin and rats to de-eyeball." He wrenched open the door, and cool spring air hit their faces.

But before they could step one foot outside, ropes slithered across the floor and coiled themselves around Kyra and Fred.

"I can't enslave you, but there's nothing in a marriage spell that says I can't *eat* you." A malicious grin spread across the witch's face.

She grabbed a cauldron off the counter behind her and draped the handle over the hook in the fireplace. "I do fancy myself a bit of tasty stew every now and then," she muttered. "But a knife won't do. . . ."

While the witch's back was turned, Kyra reached up into her shirtsleeve and slid out a swab from one of the hidden pockets in the hem. She tucked the swab under her finger, potion-damp-side out.

The witch came back with a small saw. "This should do the trick."

She raised Kyra's hand to get a good angle and then dropped it immediately after Kyra dabbed her with the swab. The saw clattered to the floor.

The witch looked between Kyra and Fred, disoriented and confused.

Kyra picked up the confusion swab, shoved it back into her sleeve, and grabbed the knife off the table. While the witch mumbled incoherently, Kyra cut the ropes holding her, and got to work on Fred.

"What's wrong with her?" he asked.

"Confusion potion—I got it from a friend." Kyra glanced at Fred to see if he bought this. "I wouldn't go wandering through the forest by myself without a little bit of protection."

"Huh," he said, but didn't say anything else as he came free. He was just in time to catch the witch as she stumbled forward. He gently lowered her to the floor.

"Stubborn thing," Kyra said, and dabbed the witch one more time with the swab to buy them a few extra minutes. Then she shooed the animals and Fred out the door.

Ten

"So, ANYTHING ELSE I should know about?" Fred asked.

They'd run for half the day, until the trees had thinned and the land turned to pasture, and toward late afternoon they'd come upon a run-down farmhouse.

There was no sign of the farmer who owned the place—the horse stable was empty and there was no carriage next to the stalls. Kyra guessed that he might be off to sell his goods at market. They were both relieved when Fred spotted an abandoned barn filled with hay on the outskirts of the farm, where they would be safely hidden should the farmer show up.

"I don't know what you're talking about." Kyra adjusted herself in the hay of the barn loft.

"Well, there's the fact that you're a witch." Fred dug around in his pack.

"Only a spark," Kyra said.

"Then there's that great trick you have up your sleeve that even a powerful witch is helpless against."

"A gift from a friend!" Kyra reminded him.

"I'm starting to think there might be more to this dairy-maid than meets the eye."

Kyra could only smile and shrug nervously. Little did he know.

"And what's up with this obeeka thing?" Fred asked.

Kyra hesitated, recalling the first time she'd met Ariana, and the stories a witch had told her of curses and monsters and evil creatures from far-off lands. *Make-believe*, Ariana had said.

"It was probably just something the witch made up to scare us," Kyra said at last.

Fred moved around to sit beside her in a patch of late-afternoon sunlight streaking in through a crack in the wall, then patted a spot on the other side of him for Langley to settle down into. The dog had been pacing uneasily since he'd been brought up the ladder steps. Rosie hadn't been doing much better. On the other side of Kyra, she was curled into a tight little ball.

Fred leaned back and propped himself on one elbow to face Kyra.

"What?" Kyra brushed the hair back from her face.

He didn't say anything, just kept watching her.

"I'm not a witch." Kyra nestled into the pile of hay beside

him. "I just have the spark, so I *could be* a witch. But I choose not to."

Fred put a bag of shaggy carrots he'd liberated from the farmer's garden between them. Kyra picked one out.

"I should have guessed you were a witch," Fred said, "from the evil eye you're always giving me."

Kyra ignored him. Rosie moved close and put her head in Kyra's lap.

"I've heard of Seers," Fred went on, pulling a carrot out and taking a big bite. "But I've never actually met one. It sounds pretty cool. Do you see the future?"

"It's not cool, and it only happened once." Thank the Goddess of Secrets she'd lied about that. "If you don't work to develop it, it goes away." Or so she'd been told. Or maybe she just hoped. She was beginning to have some doubts.

"Uh-huh."

"It's like you can see things beneath the surface. It could be things that might happen or did happen. Believe me, it's horrible. You can't make sense of what you see, and you just drive yourself crazy trying to understand the images that come to you."

"That sounds like more than once. You're using the plural."

"I was speaking in general."

"Uh-huh."

"I *was*."

"Does your family know? I mean, I've heard there's prejudice here against witches, but I think they'd want you to be who you are. Train yourself so you know how to handle your gift. That's what they do where I'm from—if you're born with the witch's spark you get training. If you don't want to work as a witch, you don't have to, but at least you know what you can do. Didn't your family encourage you at all?"

"They did." Kyra's whole body tightened.

"And?"

"I ran away."

Fred looked stunned. "You what?"

"It was a long time ago. Can we talk about something else?"

Fred still had a shocked expression on his face, but then he recovered and gave her a wicked smile. "Only if I can call you Little Witchy."

"Ha-ha." Kyra threw the frond end of the carrot she'd been eating at him.

How could Happy-Go-Lucky Fred ever understand what it was like to be born into a role you didn't want to play? A role people feared and despised? A role you weren't allowed to walk away from? Kyra'd had no choice but to run away. The Potioners' Society had been more than happy to take on an enthusiastic ten-year-old apprentice. Her parents weren't happy about it at all.

Fred lay back in the hay, arms behind his head.

Kyra tried to entice Rosie with a biscuit, but the pig just sighed and closed her eyes. "This is why I hate animals."

"Because they love you unconditionally and keep you warm at night?"

"No." Kyra rubbed the soft bristles right above the pig's snout. She hoped Rosie's nose would start working again tomorrow. "Because they can't tell you what's wrong with them, and there's nothing you can do about it."

"And you hate them for that?"

Kyra scrunched up her face. "You know what I mean."

"No, I honestly don't." Fred turned toward her. "Why do you have such a hard time letting anyone in?"

"That's not fair. I'm here with you, aren't I?"

"You didn't want to have anything to do with me when you met me, and you've continually tried to ditch me, even though you couldn't ask for a better traveling companion—"

"Except maybe someone who bathes—"

"You're giving Rosie away to some distant relative when she obviously loves you, and you change the subject whenever it gets personal. And just because I don't throw myself into every river I encounter doesn't mean I don't bathe."

"I don't need a pet and I don't need company."

"You're lying." His eyes never left her face.

"I am *not*." Kyra looked down at the pig in her lap.

She felt his eyes on her, but when she glanced up, he turned away.

"Whatever," he said. "Rosie's just scared. Hold her tonight and I'm sure she'll be fine in the morning. I'm going to go get us some water from the well."

Fred reached into his pocket and pulled out a small white flower. "They were growing next to the carrot bed." He tossed it into Kyra's lap.

The ladder creaked as Fred made his way down, and there was a muffled thump when he jumped off the last step.

Kyra picked up the flower. It was a perfect white crocus with petals arching to almost meet at the top.

As she stared at the flower, her vision darkened and she heard a rushing in her ears as the world around her receded. The flower withered, blackened, and collapsed into dust.

As quickly as it had come, the image receded, and Kyra was once again staring at a beautiful white flower. She swallowed the nausea in her throat and stroked a silky petal with one finger.

Why wouldn't the visions go away?

Since her second full vision earlier that year, she'd been having little flashes like this, short disturbing visions she couldn't control. And every one of them, large and small, was about the same thing: the death of everyone and everything around her—nothing was spared. She tried so hard to keep her Sight all boxed up inside, but a tiny flicker had gotten through, and now she couldn't seem to contain it. At least she'd been spared another full vision—for now, anyway.

Kyra decided to spy on Fred, and peeked through a crack in the barn wall. He made his slow way to the farmer's roadside well, a spring in his step. She didn't know how anyone could look happy from overhead, but he did.

And she thought she understood why. The countryside stretched in every direction—rolling hills edged by forest to the left, neatly planted rows of crops just beginning to sprout to the right, the farmer's house and animal barn distant small squares in between. As Kyra watched, the sun dipped below the trees, and warm yellow light spilled through the spaces between them. A trio of apple trees was in full bloom below, and the smell of lilacs rose up to her on a puff of wind. When she opened herself to it, the beauty of the Kingdom of Mohr never failed to take her breath away. It was a good place. And only she could save it.

She would do whatever it took to save the kingdom.

Even if it meant killing her best friend.

A splotch of green, brighter than the trees surrounding it, came into Kyra's line of sight—a person on horseback approaching the farm from the direction of the forest.

The crocus fell from Kyra's fingers as the rider drew closer. It was the Duchess Genria.

Making good time on her glossy horse, she reached the well and dismounted, approaching Fred with a friendly wave. He waved back happily, the fool.

Kyra watched as he and the duchess talked together.

It was strange watching the duchess, in her perfectly tailored velvet riding outfit, standing in the dirt talking with Fred. The sight of her made Kyra feel twelve years old again—like she was about to get a lecture about scrubbing before her lessons with the princess. Kyra was aware of every speck of dust she'd accumulated on the road, the knots in her hair, the bits of hay sticking to her clothes.

Kyra clenched her hands. If only she could keep him from saying anything stupid. If he mentioned *Kitty*. . . .

The thought sent spiders of tension crawling over her skin.

Fred was doing a lot of head-shaking and "no"-ing. That was good. The duchess wouldn't know him and certainly wouldn't know that he had anything to do with Kyra. If he was denying he was with anyone, it might be okay.

But waiting to find out was killing her.

When the duchess turned her head up sharply toward the barn, Kyra's heart stopped cold.

The noblewoman seemed to be looking right at her. It was impossible—there was no way she could see anything through a crack in a barn wall a hundred yards away and two stories up. Just as abruptly as the duchess looked up, she looked away again.

The duchess didn't seem satisfied with Fred, but she mounted her horse, wheeled it away, and galloped out of sight.

Kyra slumped down into the hay.

Below, the barn door scraped open, and Kyra heard Fred's footsteps on the ladder.

His face appeared above the edge of the loft. "Do you have any idea who I just talked to?" He didn't wait for Kyra to answer. "The queen's sister! Who, by the way, is absolutely gorgeous. She's in the area looking for a fugitive—not really what you'd expect from the queen's sister, but Mohr is a pretty strange kingdom. And a friend of hers told her about us. A *witch* friend. Can you believe it?" Fred plopped himself down. "She asked where my wife was, and I told her she must have the wrong person. It didn't really look like she believed me, but she did believe I was a complete idiot and not worth her time."

"Imagine that."

"Ha-ha." Fred slung the waterskins off his shoulder.

 105

"Wait," Kyra said, sitting up in alarm. "How did she find us? We're miles away from the witch."

"No idea."

"Fred," Kyra said tentatively, "you didn't remove anything from the witch's house, did you?"

"What do you take me for?"

Kyra cocked her head.

"She did give me some warm socks before she went and got you."

"Fred!"

"What? My feet were cold. You should have seen the holes in my other socks!"

"She put a trace on you in case you escaped. Damn." Witch's traces were much like potions tags, except that if you got rid of the object, you got rid of the trace. Nothing got rid of a potions tag.

"Really? I thought she was just worried about my feet." Fred touched one of his socks.

"Go back to the river—"

"That was a mile back!"

"—and throw the socks in. We can't have a trace on us. We don't want the duchess to come looking for us again. Next time, she'll bring the guard with her."

"Why should we be afraid of her?"

"You aren't from around here, so you might not know about the duchess. But I'm telling you, do NOT mess with her. She's powerful in the kingdom, and even though we aren't who she's looking for"—Kyra tried to make this sound as though she really believed it—"she could have us imprisoned for a long time before things got cleared up. There wouldn't need to be a reason, either—people can be thrown in prison here for irritating the wrong person."

"Hmmm . . ." Fred mused. "She is like a beautiful but poisonous flower."

"She isn't just beautiful." Kyra hesitated, but she needed to make sure Fred realized the danger they were in. "The duchess," she whispered, "is a witch."

"No way! Like Miss I'm-going-to-eat-you-in-my-stew back there?"

"No! Not like her. The duchess's gift is persuasion and attraction. It's very difficult to say no to her if she turns her gift on you. You're lucky she only put an attraction spell on you and didn't turn on the persuasion, or you would've spilled every little secret you've got."

Fred looked sincerely disturbed. He rubbed his hand over his head, rumpling his brown hair. "I didn't know."

"Please, just go down to the river, toss the socks, and avoid falling in love with any dangerous people, okay?"

"Fine." Fred's smile turned back on. "But I want you to know that I will then be completely sockless and cold."

Kyra glared at him.

"Okay. Just promise me you'll be here when I get back. I don't think we should separate the animals right now."

Kyra sighed. "I promise."

"Oh, I almost forgot." Fred reached into his pocket and tossed something over to Kyra.

On reflex, Kyra caught the object. The necklace the witch had stolen from her. "How did you . . . ?"

He put his fingers together in the two-fingered sign of a thief. "Just a small talent I picked up in my travels." He winked at her and disappeared over the side of the loft.

Eleven

THE NEXT DAY, Kyra cursed herself for not having slipped away the night before. She was tired, dirty, and completely unnerved by the appearance of the duchess.

Plus, it was raining.

That wasn't Fred's fault, but somehow it seemed everything would be easier to bear if she didn't have to share her misery with anyone.

When Fred had come back without the witch socks the night before, she'd pretended to be sleeping. She felt him lie down beside her and could have sworn he was watching her in the dark of the hayloft. Kyra hadn't dared risk opening her eyes to see. His breath fluttered against her face, and she felt the lightest touch on her cheek—something soft and warm resting there for the briefest second.

Fred had kissed her.

She heard him settle back into the hay.

She listened until she was sure he was asleep, then peeked at him. She hadn't gotten used to how beautiful he was. It still sent a jolt through her. She wanted to reach out and touch the curve of his lips.

But she didn't. Instead she'd nestled in beside him and, despite everything that had happened, fell into an easy sleep, a warm feeling inside.

Then this morning she'd awoken to the sound of rain on the roof and the animals antsy and ready to go.

Fred was unusually quiet, almost somber as they headed out.

The rain alternated between pouring and drizzling. The intense deluge made it difficult to see ahead, and the drizzling, while bearable, made Kyra irritable.

Rosie and Langley, on the other hand, were fully recovered from the incident with the witch. Rosie's nose was twitching back and forth, sniffing the ground in front of her. The rain didn't seem to have an effect on her at all.

Fred's mood sank even further as they walked.

They were getting close to Wexford. Soon there would be other people on the path. Kyra needed to put on a glamour before they encountered anyone who'd recognize her.

The time had come to lose Fred.

As Kyra debated the possible ways she could slip away, she noticed how quiet the forest had become. The rain fell

in a fine mist now, but it wasn't that. The birds that had optimistically started singing when the rain had let up were now silent.

Then she heard the faintest noise.

Someone following them.

She glanced behind, and just for a moment, there it was—a flash of black in the green behind them.

"Fred," Kyra whispered, "there's someone behind us."

"So?"

"Someone following us."

"Why would someone be following us?"

"I don't know, but it looks like someone who's up to no good. He's wearing all black."

"So," Fred replied, "are you."

"I'm wearing black because it travels well, but that's not the point. This person is dodging in and out of the trees."

"Uh-huh."

"Have you forgotten about the goblins who attacked you?"

"Do goblins wear black and dodge in and out of the trees?"

"As soon as we get around that bend"—Kyra pointed to a curve in the path in front of them—"let's step off the trail. Whether he's a robber or not, he'll pass us by and we won't have to worry about it."

"I think I can protect us against one guy." Fred crossed his arms across his chest.

"But why go to the trouble? Come on."

Around the corner, the path widened and straightened

out. Upper branches of elm trees arched overhead to create a canopy.

Kyra pushed Fred behind the wide trunk of a cedar with Rosie and Langley.

"We're going to need more cover than this." Kyra got out her potions bag. Dumping the contents into her palm, she quickly scanned for the cloaking mister.

Beside her, Fred started in surprise. "What is that?" he asked. "It's got a red skull on the label."

Kyra cringed. He *would* notice the most dangerous poison in her bag.

Shoving everything but the cloaking potion back into the bag, she shook her head and said in a quiet voice, "A friend gave me a bag of potions in case of emergencies." She took the cap off the cloaking potion. "Remember I told you about the confusion potion? I don't know what they all are."

"What sort of friend would give you a potion with a red skull on it and not tell you what it is?"

"I'm sure it's in the bag by mistake." She started spritzing the cloaking potion over each of them and the animals.

"A red skull means it's extremely dangerous, Kitty. One of my friends was a potions apprentice. So much as a tiny drop leaks out of that bottle—whatever it is—and we could all be dead."

"Shh!" They were completely coated now—she couldn't see Fred or the animals. She felt Rosie lean up against her leg.

"This stuff really works," Fred said. "Who is this friend of yours?"

"Shh!" Kyra repeated, and squeezed his arm to silence him.

In moments, the man in black came around the corner. He crouched low, scanning the ground. Kyra heard Fred's sharp intake of breath.

The man moved like a spider toward them.

Dartagn.

Still on her trail. That was bad.

Fred held Kyra tightly in his arms, so close she could feel his breath against her face.

Dartagn drew nearer.

He stopped on the path beside the fat tree they hid behind, his mustache drooping with wet, peering intently at the ground. Their footprints?

Kyra squinted. There must have been something there, or he wouldn't have been looking.

Dartagn began inching off the trail, heading toward them. He paused and stooped down, studying the earth.

Less than a foot away. If he reached out, he'd touch their legs.

He looked back up, staring blindly at where they were standing. He leaned forward, his hand reaching toward them.

Tup-tup, tup-tup. Tup-tup, tup-tup.

The sound of many feet marching came down the trail.

Dartagn paused, hand outstretched.

Abruptly, he stood and jogged off in the other direction.

Kyra relaxed into Fred's arms. Somehow, when he couldn't see her, it seemed okay to let herself lean into him. Just a little bit.

The *Tup-tup, tup-tup* grew louder.

The first soldiers came around the bend—two men across,

row after row of soldiers, until the long line of royal blue filed past Kyra and Fred. An endless procession of blue coats and black boots; glowing, poison-coated weapons strapped across their backs. A squadron of the King's Army, members of the main ground fighting force.

Finally, the last of the army marched down the trail.

Fred's forehead pressed against Kyra's, and they stood together for a moment, completely still as the *Tup-tup, tup-tup* faded.

"Why is the army patrolling the woods around Wexford, Kitty?"

"I don't know," Kyra lied, glad they were still invisible, glad he couldn't see the expression on her face.

"Why were you hiding from that man in the king's black?"

"I wasn't! It's just—he was creepy! That mustache!"

It was the last thing she said to him before she invisibly swooped down, groped for his boots, and pulled the laces loose.

As she heard him stumble and stop with a "Kitty, hold on a minute, my laces are untied," she took off running down the path, Rosie clutched in her arms.

Twelve

KYRA RAN UNTIL HER breath was short, until Rosie squirmed uncomfortably in her arms, until Fred's voice calling for her was just a small, faraway sound. Eventually she couldn't hear him at all, and she slowed her pace.

The rain began pouring down again, washing away the last remnants of the cloaking charm.

Outside the city, Kyra slipped under a large dense fir tree to wait out the downpour. Surrounded by the sharp scent of pine, she wrapped her arms around her knees, Rosie nestled between her legs and chest. The tiny pig looked up, then tucked her chin in and sighed contentedly.

Just then, the sky turned black and the rain bloodred. Where it hit the ground, dark pools of coppery blood steadily rose until they filled Kyra's vision. She coughed, choking on the bloody mist in the air. And then, in moments, the rain disappeared again. Just as all her other flashes of Sight had.

Kyra covered her eyes and slumped against the tree. The bloody scene revealed in her Sight hadn't taken place yet—and she had to make sure it never did. That's why she would do anything she had to—even abandon a new friend, even kill an old friend—to stop her vision from coming true.

It rained through the rest of the day, and when it stopped, Kyra decided she might as well stay where she was for the night. She was tired and felt hollowed out. Let the King's Army, Dartagn, and Fred get ahead while she rested.

The path to Wexford was crowded enough right now without her.

Kyra sank into a fitful sleep under the tree, holding tight to the warm pig in her arms.

In the morning, the sun crept up into a clear blue sky. Today could be the day when Rosie led her to where the princess was hiding.

Kyra was ready for the whole thing to be over.

She spritzed on an old lady glamour, feeling her body contort to take on the new shape. The Master Trio's glamours were the real deal—they didn't just alter the way people saw you, they altered reality itself for the short time they were effective. Kyra even felt the weight of her enormous old lady bosoms as she leaned forward to pick up Rosie's leash.

She gave Rosie the lead. They padded softly through the rain-damp forest, then onto a main road into the city. No one paid attention to them. They were was just an old lady and a pig.

The closer they got to the city, the more people filled the road, and their pace grew slower and slower. When a wagon full of jugglers joined them, Kyra realized why the road was so crowded: April 30, Beltane Eve, was the next day. It was a huge spring festival that brought people to Wexford from all around the kingdom, to be entertained or to be the entertainers.

The jugglers kept up their act the entire way to the city, stealing caps from kids, tossing them into a bright arc of balls and pins and knives, and then deftly plopping them back on heads and shouting out, "Winegarten Jugglers! Everyone, come see us at the fairgrounds!"

It annoyed Kyra no end.

The dirt road slowly gave way to cobblestones, and buildings rose up on all sides as they entered the city proper.

Wexford.

Kyra had missed the capital after she'd moved to Trent to form the Master Trio—she really had. There was so much going on all the time, and the market was ten times bigger than the one in Trent. And this was where her best friend, Ari, the princess, lived.

Ari was irreplaceable—no one laughed as easily or as hard as she did, or knew exactly what Kyra needed—oftentimes even before Kyra knew herself. Leaving Ari behind had been, by far, the most difficult part about moving to Trent. But Kyra had thrown herself into her work, and that had filled the hole that had opened up in her.

Most of the time, anyway.

The castle came into view, high upon the hill at the far edge of the city, and Kyra's heart skipped a beat.

She'd been happy enough in Trent. Until three months before, when her first horrifying vision had come—a sight so grim that it drove Kyra to abandon her life as a master potioner and journey back to Wexford in time for Ariana's fifteenth birthday bash. The party at which Kyra had toasted the princess, then calmly reached down, pulled a poisoned needle out of a disguised holster, and sent it flying across the room, targeted directly at her best friend's heart.

And missed. Kyra *never* missed.

The needle thunked into the chair beside Ariana's neck, and instead of collapsing to the floor, the princess had let out an ear-piercing scream. The entire ballroom had erupted into panic.

Kyra had run for her life, chased by cries of "Assassin!" from the crowd, Ariana's scream ringing through her head.

She had fled to her concealed hideaway—her secret hut in the woods—and lain low for a month, too terrified and too angry at herself for her failure—to venture forth.

Now Kyra had returned in the glamour of a dumpy old lady, led by a pig on a leash.

The closer they got to the castle gleaming in the midday sun, the more intent Rosie grew on her hunt, until suddenly, nose pressed to the ground, she yanked Kyra off onto a side street.

The pig's nose quivered with an intensity Kyra had never

seen before. Rosie tugged hard on the lead, pulling Kyra through the winding mews of the city.

Soon they were going in the opposite direction of the palace—to the market and shop-lined streets of the northwest district.

To the Sleepy Boar Inn. It was a three-story yellow eyesore that slumped against the building beside it as though it were tired.

Rosie pulled Kyra right through the gateway of the courtyard and began digging at the front door. Kyra pressed the latch down and pushed it open.

The concierge stand to her left was empty, but she could hear a voice down the hall. ". . . wake-up service is available," the man was saying, "and if you need anything else . . ."

Rosie pulled her straight ahead to the stairs. Kyra followed in a rush, hoping they got out of view before the concierge returned.

They flew up the stairs, Kyra's old-lady bones complaining with each step.

At the third-story landing, Rosie led Kyra down the corridor to the right and stopped in front of a door with *302* painted in gold letters.

"Good girl, Rosie," Kyra whispered. Her heart beat wildly. Could Ariana really be on the other side of this door? It would be genius of the royal family to hide their daughter away in an unassuming inn so close to home.

But it felt wrong somehow. Not the way the monarchy usually worked. They never did anything that smart.

Kyra got her weapons ready, one quill dipped in deadly, blue phosphorescent Peccant Pentothal, another half dozen tipped with Doze. Putting her ear to the door, she listened for sounds of guards inside. There would be at least one protecting the princess, possibly more.

Silence.

Strange. But a well-made muffling potion could cloak a whole roomful of soldiers.

Kyra gently tried the handle. Unlocked. She turned the knob and pushed the door open.

Inside was nothing like Kyra expected.

No one was there. The shades were drawn and dust motes floated in the shafts of light that filtered through. The bed was made and the nightstand held only a lantern. A large traveling case sat in the corner, and a heap of shabby clothes lay on the floor.

She sniffed. The room smelled strangely like Newman House. Or at least like it had when Kyra had last been there, hiding out on the floor of the hermit's flat.

Sort of musty and old-mannish.

Rosie went and sat down on the pile of clothes in an incredibly self-satisfied way. Her nose had most definitely stopped twitching.

Kyra shut the door behind her. "Rosie, you haven't found me a person at all," she said as she began combing the room for signs of the princess. She wrenched open the nightstand drawer. "I thought Katzenheim pigs found *people*. You've just found me a room. Some old man's room."

Which is when she realized that they were not, in fact, alone.

Because the pile of clothes Rosie was sitting on started moving and let out a horrifying scream as the old man lying there discovered a pig staring down at him.

Kyra calmly pocketed her killing quill but kept a Doze-tipped needle at the ready.

The man dragged himself across the floor, trying to shake off the pig. "What are you doing in my room?"

"What are you doing on the floor?" Kyra demanded.

She looked the man full in the face. And almost fell over in surprise.

No wonder this room smelled like Newman House. This guy *was* the hermit of Newman House. Ellie.

Ellie the hermit tried to stand up. "Get this blasted thing off of me!"

Kyra grabbed Rosie with one hand, and with the other reached into the basket and unpinned the small piece of fabric so that the pig wouldn't keep trying to sit on what it believed was its quarry.

Ellie got to his feet and dusted himself off. "Who in tarnation are *you*?"

It took Kyra a moment to remember he was seeing her old-lady glamour.

If he didn't know who she was, she didn't have anything to lose by asking a few questions. "Where's the princess?"

"The *princess*? What in the world are you talking about?"

"You know, the daughter of the king and queen? This pig

was supposed to lead me to her. Imagine how disappointing it is to be led to you instead."

"I don't have any money or anything to steal, if that's what you're getting at. Ellie's never gotten any favors from the monarchy," he said, gesturing to himself. "I just want to be left alone. Why can't I just be left alone?"

He began muttering to himself.

Kyra watched him closely. Could he be Ariana in a glamour? Some sort of personality-affecting glamour? No—this was the same Ellie she remembered from the occasional glimpses at Newman House, even down to the nervous nose-picking.

Was there something here she was missing?

She picked up Rosie and looked down at the little pink pig. Rosie looked back at her with innocent eyes.

Arlo.

Kyra had made a huge mistake.

Thirteen

THE PIG HAD NEVER been set to find the princess. Arlo Abbaduto had been playing a game with her.

Kyra didn't know why she was surprised. Sure, killing the princess would have helped Arlo—by plunging the kingdom into chaos, leaving it vulnerable to the King of Criminals. But more than that, he probably hungered for Kyra to fail and be captured. Arlo's revenge on her.

Not because she and the Master Trio had turned down his request for potions.

But because of what she'd done the second time they'd met.

It was a full year after their first meeting, and Kyra had been summoned to the castle by the king. When she'd arrived, she was immediately ushered into a small meeting room with His Majesty, the vials she'd been told to bring gently clinking in her bag.

The king had a gentle look when he wasn't making speeches. A smile flickered across his face as Kyra came into the room, the laugh lines around his eyes deepening. He sat in a high-backed oak chair at a glossy wooden table, a stack of documents in front of him.

"You know what I've asked you to come here for," he said.

"Not exactly, sire."

He leaned forward, his elbows on the table. "We have a chance to put a dangerous criminal leader behind bars for life. Or to execute him."

"Arlo Abbaduto?"

"We suspect he orchestrated the killing of—" The king rubbed a hand over his sandy beard, now speckled with gray. "Never mind that. The important thing is that Arlo chose truth serum over a trial."

Kyra watched the expression on the king's face harden, the lines of his face growing stern. "He must assume we will use the Cera Truth Serum," said the king. "It's been a gift to innocent people. It spares them a long and complicated trial."

"But you believe Arlo's procured something to block the Cera Serum."

The king nodded. "He is too confident. And he has the resources."

Kyra looked down at her hands.

The king continued. "Which is where you come in. Your potion—what do you call it?"

"*Poison*, Your Majesty. I call it poison. It is an experimental solution that—"

He waved her off. "Yes, yes, but what are you calling it?"

"Red Skull Serum. So as not to forget how *deadly* it is, my lord."

The king ignored her emphasis on the lethality of the serum. "You know how dangerous the man is. This opportunity to put him away, we cannot pass this up just because—"

"Because the Red Skull Serum might kill him."

"He wouldn't show us the same mercy." The king lightly tapped the stack of papers in front of him. "Arlo is not expecting us to have any tricks up our sleeve. He's going to tie his own noose, Kyra, when he gets some Red Skull Serum into him."

"It may kill him."

The king smiled. "A risk I'm willing to take."

But it was Kyra who was going to have to be there to watch the entire thing. Only she would be able to get the dilution exactly right, to make sure the truth didn't kill the person.

Soon Kyra was following a guard down to the dungeons. A scribe was already waiting in the cell, paper and quill on the table in front of him. Arlo was to his right, his arms chained to the table. The manacles were huge—they didn't look like the kind normally used for humans.

He'd grinned when he saw her, a wicked smile that

stretched his toady face. "If it isn't the *Master Potioner*. Too good to sell me potions, but not too good to use them on me?" He rattled his chains.

Kyra was rattled too. She refused to look at him as she sat down and placed her potions bag on the table. She could feel him staring as she went through the process of diluting the phosphorescent poison to turn it into her Red Skull Serum.

It wasn't until she touched the single drop of serum on his hand that she met his gaze.

He half lowered his lids over his eyes. "You think you've got me, girlie. But you don't."

Kyra packed up her potions as the scribe began questioning Arlo, a bad feeling tingeing her movements.

It was an honest mistake.

Ever since then, Kyra had been exceedingly careful about labeling *everything* in her potions bag, not just the poisons—working her crabbed handwriting onto each label until no one could mistake an unlabeled vial for the wrong solution.

She learned later that Ned had been using the solutions in her kit. He was always needing an extra element for a potion, and too lazy to go to the cabinet—not when Kyra's bag was right there under her workbench, handy and well stocked. As usual, he'd been sloppy about putting things back where they belonged, and he had accidentally replaced her brown bottle of dilution medium with a nearly identical vial of essential pine oils.

By the time Kyra realized her mistake, it was too late.

Arlo had gone rigid, gasping, flinging his arms out so

stiffly that they'd snapped the chain linking his manacles to the table.

And then he'd fallen over onto the ground, blind, and his breath so shallow that Kyra wasn't sure he was breathing at all. She'd pressed her ear to his sweaty face and heard nothing, then pulled a mirror from her bag and held it against his open mouth.

The faintest fogging against the glass.

"Has he turned to . . . wood?" the scribe asked in a horrified whisper.

Kyra sat back on her heels and looked at Arlo, and indeed he looked like a wooden statue of himself. Whatever the mixture was that she'd created, it had given his skin a yellow, grainy texture like polished pine. He was cool to the touch, too, like a well-carved dummy.

"What have you done?" the scribe said.

"Nothing I can't undo," Kyra had replied with more conviction than she felt. And then she got to work.

The next two hours were spent administering every healing potion Kyra knew, plus other remedies people found in medicinal books.

She'd saved him. He'd lost all of his hair, and his eyes had bulged out and never gone back to normal, but nonetheless, Kyra had managed to resuscitate him. She recorded her mistake in her notes and forgot about it. By that evening, he was conscious again, though looking like someone who'd been to death's door and back.

Through it all, Arlo had maintained his innocence. And

true to the letter of the law—and no longer trusting Kyra to get the truth from Arlo—the king released him.

Arlo had joked about it. "Well, *Master Potioner*, I don't know whether I should thank you or put a contract on your head. It seems I owe you my near-death *and* my life."

"Maybe the two acts cancel each other out?"

"Maybe." Arlo's smile had been mirthless. "I suppose you'll find out one day."

That day had come.

Kyra felt like a fool. A complete and utter fool. How could she have been so stupid as to go to Arlo for help? To believe he'd forgive and forget?

Kyra sank down onto the bed. *Disappointment* didn't begin to describe the feeling flooding her—it was like someone had filled her insides with heavy, sticky glue. Her search for the princess was nowhere.

A sense of urgency filled her. Kyra needed to get out of the hermit's room and back to finding the princess. "Come on," she said to the pig in her arms. "We're leaving."

Ellie was still on the floor, grumbling and picking invisible bugs off himself as Kyra departed.

Hearing the voice of the concierge, she stopped at the top of the stairs.

"No, fold them this way! If you fold them like that, they're going to be horribly wrinkled! Our customers don't want wrinkled pillowcases."

Kyra waited while the concierge continued to explain how to fold linens. Apparently, this new person needed to know every little detail about folding every type of fabric that could ever possibly be used in an inn. When at last she heard the sound of the cart rolling down the hall, Kyra dashed out the door with Rosie in her arms.

How much time before it was too late to kill the princess and save the kingdom? She had no idea. Kyra needed a new strategy, and she needed one fast.

She had to get out of town. Wexford had never seemed like a likely place to find the princess, and it was the most dangerous place Kyra could be.

But first she had to find a family who would take Rosie as a pet. Kyra had a job to do, and she couldn't be weighed down with an animal that needed care and feeding. She stopped at the Saturday market.

The towheaded little girl at the fruit stand promised to take care of her and to bring her everywhere with her. "Maybe she'll like jugglers and carnival games, and even fair candy!" the girl said, eyes round and eager. Kyra wasn't sure pigs liked fair candy or carnival games, but at least it sounded like Rosie would have a happy-ish life.

As happy as a pig could be while living with a little girl.

Rosie was a tool whose purpose had been to lead her to the princess, nothing more. If Kyra felt a sinking feeling in her stomach as she handed over Rosie's leash—well, it was something she'd have to ignore.

After buying some food and quickly refreshing her old-lady glamour, Kyra made her way out of the city. As she trudged down the majestic evergreen-lined road, alongside those departing Wexford, she did her best not to walk half bent over as the full weight of her failure descended on her. She had no idea what to do next. Contacting Arlo had been a last resort.

She had been walking on the road for a good hour when she remembered: 07 211, Peccant Pentothal. What had that potion been doing in Ellie's apartment?

Kyra stopped in her tracks, almost falling flat on her face as the people behind crashed into her. She stepped to the side to get out of the way.

What if her pig *hadn't* been misled by Arlo? What if Rosie *had* taken her to the owner of the piece of cloth in her basket—not its first owner, but its most recent one? It was just too much of a coincidence that Ellie had the poison in his flat *and* that the Katzenheim pig had led her to him. Had Ellie somehow gotten a piece of Ariana's clothing? How? Why? How was the hermit mixed up in all this?

And he'd acted so weird. Ellie had to know something he hadn't told her. How could she have let him slip away like that? And who was he really? His antisocial tendencies took on a new, more sinister edge. He'd always seemed perfectly harmless. A little odd and grumpy, sure, but . . .

Kyra turned back toward town, slipping between the carts and foot traffic, walking twice as fast as she had on her way out.

At the Sleepy Boar, she snuck past the concierge and his new assistant and lumbered back upstairs to 302. She knocked, and when no one answered, she opened the door.

The room was completely empty. No pile of old-man clothes, and no Ellie the hermit, either.

Kyra ran down the stairs and stopped at the front desk. The concierge, his wispy hair combed over the top of his head, glanced up from a pile of papers and squinted at her. His face was wrinkly and old, but it was the dark purple droops under his eyes that caught Kyra's attention. He looked like he hadn't slept in days. "May I help you?" He adjusted his half-spectacles.

"Yes, I'm looking for the, uh, gentleman in 302."

"I'm pretty sure"—the clerk ruffled through his papers— "that he's checked out."

Of course he had, because he knew someone was after him.

Kyra had never felt so stupid in her entire life.

"We're family, and I have an urgent message for him."

"You're his family?" The clerk looked genuinely confused. "He told me that he was all alone in the world. He said it often."

"He exaggerates," Kyra said, improvising. "I'm his cousin. Second cousin. Or third."

The clerk was watching her. "If you say so."

"I really do need to speak with him. . . . Do you know where he went?"

The concierge's assistant, a young man close to Kyra's real age and a bit broad around the shoulders for desk work, had crept up. He now waited at his boss's elbow, staring at Kyra.

The concierge turned to him. "Dulo, did you fold all the towels the way I showed you?"

"Yes."

Kyra could feel the assistant staring at her. When she met his eyes, they seemed to grow black. She blinked, and when she opened her lids, saw only the assistant's gray eyes looking at her curiously

"Good. Now, please tally our receipts for yesterday." The concierge handed the assistant a small book with papers sticking out, then shrugged at Kyra. "Sorry, but I'm afraid the guest you're looking for—your *cousin*—didn't leave a forwarding address. Maybe he went home?"

"Maybe! Thank you," she said, turning to the door.

Kyra walked away from the inn with a horrible buzzing in her head.

There was no way Ellie the hermit had gone back home to Newman House. Not if he was involved with hiding the princess.

Kyra had been so close. She could just kick herself. How could she have been so dumb?

She needed to find Ellie. And Ariana. Or both. Which meant she needed Rosie back.

There was nothing else but to yank Rosie away from the little girl she'd left her with.

Except that she couldn't even do that.

By the time she got to the market, the daytime stalls had closed up and the evening vendors were moving into their places. The fruit stand was gone, and the Saturday market wouldn't be back for another week.

Frantic, Kyra ran down the length of the street searching for any sign of the girl or her family. The street ended in a city park with a giant fountain in the middle. Kyra sat down heavily beside it. This was hopeless. Although . . .

She jumped up. There was one last chance.

Juggler, carnival games, and *fair candy* echoed through Kyra's head. The little girl had mentioned all of them. Which could mean only one thing: she'd be going to the festival.

In the distance was a sparkling of twinkling lights, and as Kyra drew close to the fairgrounds, she could smell the savory-sweet scent of roasting meat, fried bread, and caramel. Inside the gate there were jugglers surrounded by children; donkeys with children riding on top of them; throwing games with lines of children eagerly waiting for their turn; and children battling each other with giant turkey legs as weapons at the food carts.

Children were everywhere. And at least a third of them were blond. Just like the little market girl. The crowds were so thick that she had no hope of spotting Rosie's pink face.

So Kyra would have to check each one. She pushed into the crowd by the jugglers, grabbing and spinning each blond child around as she worked her way down the line. No little market girl. Next was the donkey ring—no luck there. By the time Kyra reached the food stalls, children were squealing and running to avoid her. One brave boy poked her with a turkey leg and shouted, "Get off!" when she spun his little sister around.

She was never going to find the market girl. Or Rosie.

In desperation, she turned at last to the lines for the

outhouses—the smell wafting from that direction was less than appealing, but Kyra couldn't let that deter her. Hustling her old bones, she shoved into the crowd, raising a bunch of shouts and curses in her wake.

That's when she overheard it. A little girl voice that sounded familiar.

"Mum, I don't feel good. I'm *never* eating so much fair candy again."

Kyra spotted the girl from the market standing with her mum.

Rosie was nowhere in sight. So much for sharing her fair candy. No wonder the girl felt sick.

"Excuse me," Kyra said. "I'm looking for Rosie—my pig?"

The girl immediately burst into tears. "I coulda shared my treats with *her*," she wailed.

The girl's mother looked uncomfortable. "I'm sorry, ma'am. It was too good of an offer. We don't make so much at our stand that we can turn down good money like that."

"What are you talking about?"

"We sold her."

"Can you tell me who you sold her to?"

Please don't say the butcher, please don't say the butcher, please, please, not the butcher.

"Well, he seemed like a nice young man."

"Did you get a name?"

"I didn't catch his name, sorry, ma'am." The woman looked sincerely apologetic. "He seemed to know the pig and wanted her so much. . . ."

Kyra shut her eyes for a moment, wishing that somehow there was a different annoying pig lover in the world. "Rumply brown hair?" she asked, dreading the answer. "Green eyes, kind of gold in the light?"

"That's him exactly!" the woman said, happy and relieved that Kyra knew who she was talking about. "Good-looking fellow too."

Fourteen

FRED!

He'd been nothing but a pain in Kyra's behind since she'd met him. And now he had her pig. How he could tell one pig from another she didn't know. Though she had to admit Rosie did have a distinctive way about her. He probably hadn't gone far. Not with the big festival tomorrow. Beltane Eve was almost impossible to resist.

On Beltane Eve, the most festive celebration of the year, kids dressed up as horrors to scare the cold of winter back into hiding. They wandered the city all day, eating sweets and playing games. When it got dark, there was a solemn parade in honor of the dead Winter King, but once the straw-stuffed

Winter King effigy was alight on the bonfire, the kids were sent to bed and things really got rowdy, with dancing until dawn.

Kyra decided to switch glamours—if she ran across Ellie while she was looking for Fred, she didn't want him to recognize her as the old woman who'd broken into his hotel room. Who knew how the possibly evil old hermit would react? Better to keep her problems separate. Fred first, then Ellie. Her new glamour was a round-cheeked young blond woman, looking every bit the dairymaid Kyra had pretended to be earlier.

But searching for Fred and Ellie would have to wait: Kyra's eyelids were drooping from fatigue. She decided to call it a night and start fresh the next day.

She checked into a second-floor room at an inn called the Winged Dragon and took a long bath, the hot steam enshrouding her and seeming to clean away months on the road. Then she crawled into her first real bed in ages, the mattress so light and fluffy that she slid directly into a deep sleep.

The early morning sounds of the city through her window woke her all too soon.

Kyra could smell fresh bread baking somewhere, mixed with the scent of spring blossoms growing in the box outside her window. The bed was so unbelievably wonderful—she rubbed her feet under the sheets, reveling in the feel of her clean body against clean linens.

A brisk knock sounded on her door.

Kyra jumped up and realized she'd washed away the milk-maid glamour. Frantically, she looked around for her potions bag, but realized there was no time for that. Draping her sheet over her head and wrapping the rest of the cloth around her body, she stepped to the door and opened it a crack.

A maid was walking away down the hall. At Kyra's feet was a basket filled with something wrapped in cloth, which smelled tantalizingly good. Kyra put her hand on the bundle. Still warm.

What a wonderful, wonderful woman to have brought this to her. Kyra felt a giggle coming on. Warm baked goods. Breakfast!

She brought the basket back to bed with her. After polishing off two blueberry muffins, a crescent-shaped almond pastry, and two chunks of brown bread spread with butter, Kyra toyed with the idea of staying there forever—snuggled into bed, living off the delightful things that would come to her door every morning.

But no: it was time to get back to the real world and find Fred. And her pig.

Kyra put on her dairymaid glamour and hit the streets. She walked from one end of Wexford to the other—checking every shop she thought might appeal to Fred, watching outside of inns, peeking in pub windows.

Around noon, Kyra made her way to the central park for a break. The smell of hot savory pastries wafted from a stand near the fountain. She bought two fist-sized pies stuffed with new potatoes, peas, and spices, and sat down on a bench to eat them.

Streets led away from the park like spokes on a wheel, and Kyra had a view of the open-air market and the shop-lined street. She watched the ebb and flow of people as she finished her first pastry. She was feeling drowsy in the sun, her belly full, her eyes threatening to close. But they widened when she saw a man with two animals—a small pink pig and a wolflike dog.

Fred.

He had a loaf of bread under one arm and a shopping bag in the other. Kyra rose and followed him. Despite her dairy-maid glamour, she tried to be as inconspicuous as possible.

Fred turned and went inside an inn called the Thorny Rose. The place was nicer than she expected of Fred. But not so nice that it would be difficult to break into. Kyra watched the dark empty windows until a small pink pig face appeared in one of them, then turned to go.

She'd wait until that night to steal Rosie. Surely, even Fred wouldn't be dim enough to bring a pig to the parade.

Her glamour fading, she went back to her inn for a nice afternoon nap. It was going to be a long night. And she had to take advantage of that soft mattress while she could.

At dusk she peeked out the second-story window of her room. The streets were filled with people in costumes—that, she expected. What she was surprised to see, however, were soldiers in full military gear. She'd never seen soldiers decked out for combat at a festival.

Why would they be so heavily armed on Beltane Eve? Were they looking for her?

Then she spotted a man in black on a street corner: Dartagn. And the man Dartagn was talking to—the too-handsome face and perfectly coifed black hair were unmistakable.

Kyra ducked down under the windowsill for the space of two breaths. Then she peeked over again.

Her mind hadn't been playing tricks on her: it was Hal. What was he doing here? And why was he in such deep conversation with the black-clad elite soldier?

Ned came out of the pub behind them, a turkey leg in one hand, and joined in the conversation.

The remaining two members of the Master Trio of Potioners were here. And they were working with Dartagn.

Kyra tried to get a grip on herself. There was no way they could have tracked her here. If they had, surely they would have found her already. More likely they'd lost her in the forest and had come to Wexford in case she showed up.

Did the Master Trio and the King's Army think she would plan an assassination on Beltane Eve? Did that mean the princess *was* in the city?

Kyra needed that pig.

When she checked again a few minutes later, they were gone. But in their place were three shrieking little girls. One was dressed as a lady ghost with white powder dusted all over her, and the second was a thief in raggedy clothing.

They pointed at another girl and shouted, "You've got the scariest costume ever!"

"Oh my God, it's soooo creepy!"

Kyra leaned out the window for a better look at this Beltane horror and gasped.

The little girl they were pointing at was dressed in black from head to toe, with long curly black hair, and her face made up into a grimace. Eerie green potion bottles dangled from her wrist and belt. "Watch out!" the girl in black shouted. "The Princess Killer is going to get you!" She lunged at her friends and they ran off screaming.

Kyra's stomach twisted.

The horror was her.

She sat down hard on the soft bed. She'd become a scary costume.

Not exactly how she had expected her life to turn out.

Wherever he was, Fred must be seeing the same thing. Was there any possible way he could miss the connection between the Princess Killer costumes and Kyra?

Right then, more than anything, she just wanted to run away from it all.

But she couldn't. She didn't have time to even entertain the fantasy of running away. What she needed was to go get Rosie and pick up the hunt again.

First, she had to find something that *truly* belonged to the princess. Luckily, Kyra had a good idea of *exactly* where she could track down such a thing. The tailor's.

But she'd have to wait until nightfall, when all the shops were closed up tight.

Kyra reapplied her wholesome dairymaid glamour and went out.

The crowds had grown but were mostly subdued, lining

 141

the sides of the streets and waiting for the yearly processional of the straw-stuffed Winter King and the Cherry Blossom Princess, a local girl chosen for the role. An honor guard of drunken men and saucy ladies-in-waiting would make its slow way through the city, collecting revelers in its wake, until reaching a fir tree–encircled clearing at the city's outskirts. There, the Cherry Blossom Princess would light the Beltane bonfire and her guard would throw in the figure of the Winter King.

Kyra found the perfect spot: a seat in a cozy pub near the parade route. Through the wide-open double doors was a view of the main street.

She sat at the end of the bar, ordered dinner and a mug of hot cider, and settled down for an evening of people-watching. Steaming plates of food appeared in front of her, and the heady aroma of parsley butter wafting off the peas and mashed potatoes almost made her swoon face-forward into her meal.

And then she saw something that *did* make her duck down: right outside the window was Hal.

This was ridiculous. She was wearing a glamour. It didn't matter who saw her.

Still, she kept an eye on Hal and was relieved when he finally walked away.

By the time Kyra finished eating, CLOSED signs had appeared in shop windows up and down the street.

She worked her way through the throngs of people waiting for the Beltane Eve parade, and took a left down a side alley.

Unless memory failed her, this was the way to the tailor's secret back-door entrance.

It was, in fact, the only way Kyra—or Ariana—had ever gone inside.

Ariana and Kyra's adventures outside the palace had taken a toll on their clothes. But it would not do for the princess—or the princess's best friend—to be seen entering a tailor's with a stack of ripped and muddied dresses and trousers. And though Ariana had a coterie of dressmakers and seamstresses at the palace, they would all make a fuss about any damage to her clothes. How on earth could she have gotten those stains when she was supposed to have been in the palace studying with Kyra all afternoon?

So Kyra and Ariana had found someone to help them out.

The tailor at Gabrielle's Fine Dresses had no problem taking up their cause. Or their coin. Within a few months, Ariana was given her own locked closet, under the name Choizie Laurent.

The princess had never stopped using Gabrielle's. Even when the "cosmetics lessons" from Kyra ended, and their adventures became fewer and further between, Ariana had always needed someone she could trust outside the palace to repair the questionable damage that always seemed to befall her clothes.

Kyra just hoped that Ari had left something behind for Rosie's basket. Gabrielle's would definitely be easier to break into than the palace.

In the darkened alley, Kyra came upon the dress store's back entrance.

She blew Release powder into the lock. She heard something give way inside, but when she tried the door it held firm. Strange.

Taking a quill from her holster coated with a strong dose of Melt elixir, she slipped it into the crack between the doors and ran it up and down in a steady line over the bolt. The metal softened beneath the quill until finally her needle snapped through in a clean break. She pushed again and the door opened.

She snuck inside, closing the door behind her. The dark room smelled like clothes pressed with wood-fired irons, fabric glue, and raw silk.

There was something creepy about Gabrielle's Fine Dresses at night. The wooden mannequins stared at Kyra with their blank painted eyes, and shadows and light from the paradegoers' torches outside rippled and pooled in the bolts of fabric lying across the worktables. Everything seemed to be constantly moving and changing.

Kyra went through the curtain into the back room, where the row of closets for special customers was located. The only light now came from Hal's necklace around her neck.

The tiny glow was enough to shed a soft light on the closet-lined room. The half-open door to the side led to a storeroom, where a pile of mannequins lay stacked on the floor like bodies. Kyra shivered. They looked even creepier than when they were dressed and on display in the store.

Hastily, she turned to the row of closets and found the one with CHOIZIE LAURENT printed in small cursive lettering above it.

Inside hung a green wedding dress.

It had been ripped to shreds.

Fifteen

ARIANA'S WEDDING DRESS. For her arranged marriage to a man she'd never met and was certain to hate.

Ariana did not want to marry at all.

"Where would *I* be if I hadn't married, Ariana?" her mother had insisted. "Do you think I could run both the country and the King's Army? The country needs two rulers. That's the way it is."

Ariana argued that she could rule alone with trusted advisers at her side, and that even if she *did* marry, she wanted to choose the man. Anyway, there was absolutely no reason why some stranger should be king just because he was married to her.

But the queen had only shaken her head. "This idea that you might not get married at all? Nonsense. You're a royal; the land *requires* your marriage. The Nuptial Bond ceremony binds a ruler not only to her partner but to the land itself. A marriage contract is powerful magic, Ariana. It means you belong to someone."

Exactly what Ariana didn't want.

Which was why the plaintive letter from Ariana a month before her coming-of-age birthday was such a surprise.

My dearest Kitty,

The end of the world has come: my hand is being taken in marriage—against my will! But not until June. There is still time to make mother see reason. Please hasten to the palace to help me persuade her.

And to celebrate my birthday—possibly my last as a single woman.

I remain

Stubbornly yours,

Ariana

Kyra had dropped everything and rushed to Wexford. The horse couldn't go fast enough over the ice-covered roads.

When Kyra arrived, she'd found the palace bustling with wedding preparations, even though the wedding itself wasn't for months. Workmen with ladders and seamstresses carrying large bolts of fabric dashed through the halls in every direction, barely dodging one another.

Kyra ducked off the main halls and into the kitchens.

As soon as she walked through the heavy swinging doors, she was enveloped in the rich scents of simmering stew and cinnamon apples baking. Her stomach growled.

"Kyra!" shouted out the head cook. She wiped her hands on her apron, then reached up to kiss Kyra's cheeks. "Thank God!"

"It's nice to see you too, Sofie." Kyra hugged the cook, one of her favorite people at the castle. Sofie had the red-cheeked, breathless, jovial manner of someone who cooked and ate for a living, but she was rail thin and bony—the skinniest fat person Kyra had ever met. "I got a note from Ari. She sounds desperate."

"Insufferable, more like." The cook shook her head. "Haven't heard howling and carrying on like this since back before, when they locked her up 'for her health'! *Pfft.*" Sofie blew through her lips. "Kid was so healthy she managed to destroy her entire bedroom. Twice. I think back then the Little Highness just needed to get rid of some extra energy." Sofie folded her arms over the front of her apron.

"Well, try to see it from Ariana's perspective," Kyra said. "It's like being locked up in her bedroom again, isn't it? They're forcing her into something against her will. She's suffocating."

"It could be worse," Sofie said, pushing a tray of the princess's favorite raspberry-jam cookies into Kyra's hands. "I hear the prince they chose is from Lantana, and everyone says he's a nice guy. It could have been Prince Pompous from Lexeter."

"Prince Pompadou?" Kyra asked as she mounted the servants' stair. "The one who came sniffing around last spring?"

"Pompadou, Pompous Arse—whatever he goes by."

Kyra laughed.

What in the world could she do to make things better? She knew how stubborn Ariana could be. It didn't matter if it was a nice prince or a puffed-up dunderhead—Ariana knew her own mind. Kyra was pretty sure that cookies weren't going to change it.

Kyra was right to be worried.

She opened the door to find the princess pacing angrily, ripping up a piece of paper and throwing it on the floor. The mass of frizzy hair that had replaced the ringlets of her childhood bounced around Ariana's face as she stomped back and forth across the room.

Ariana had grown up to become a strong young woman. She was athletic and tough and such crazy-unpredictable fun that the stable boys all vied to be her escort when she went riding. It hurt Kyra to see her like this—angry and disheveled with tear tracks down her cheeks.

"Kitten, you came!" Kyra was swept up in a hug almost before she could set the tray on a small table inside the door. She caught a glimpse of the words CORDIALLY INVITED on one of the scraps of paper.

The princess pulled away and sat on her bed with a thump. "This is so awful, Kitty. I swore I would NOT let them do this to me. And somehow they have. My life is over."

"Ari, it might not be as bad as you think." This prompted an icy blue-eyed glare, so Kyra quickly added, "Or it might. But, Ari"—Kyra brushed her friend's hair back over her shoulders and tried for a wry smile—"never forget that your best friend is one of the world's experts in poison. There's not a man who can stand in your way. Not for long, anyway."

Ariana's cheeks lifted in a smile. "That's exactly why I wanted you to come."

"Wait, *what*? You want me to kill this guy?"

Ariana rolled her eyes. "No. Because you can make me laugh even as my life is ending."

"Well, good. It's nice to know I'm useful for more than just offing people." Kyra sat beside her on the bed. "Have you considered that getting married might be sort of fun? I was a bit doubtful at first too, but I'm starting to look forward to it."

"That's different. You got to choose who you're going to marry. If I hear one more time about how important my marriage is for the kingdom, or the words 'Nuptial Bond,' I'm going to scream." The princess's voice turned small. "What if he's all proper and everything? I might never get to go outside again. Lots of royal people NEVER leave the castle except a few times a year in a carriage. Kitty, I seriously couldn't take it."

"I know, Ari." Kyra knew how lucky she was to be marrying a man she loved. "We'll just have to figure out a way—"

"A way for me not to get married?"

Just then, a knock came at the door, and at Ari's response, in walked two dressmaker's apprentices. They swept by the girls, curtsying as they went, hung up what they were carrying, and silently departed.

It was a dress, truly one of the most beautiful wedding dresses Kyra had ever seen.

It was obvious that it had been made with love—and with this particular princess in mind. The dress didn't have a single puffy ornamental bit on it. It was a long and silky green, with a small pinecone clasp holding the material together at one shoulder. Slits were shaped into each side, as though the dressmakers had anticipated the bride's need to be free and unrestricted, able to run and move easily. The long, flowy shape was a perfect complement to Ariana's athletic frame.

It was a dress fit for the Goddess of the Hunt, running barefoot in the moonlight.

"I love it," Kyra said, before she could stop herself.

There was a horrible look on Ariana's face. She quietly nibbled and swallowed a bite of cookie. "Need tea," she mumbled.

Kyra's trip downstairs to the kitchen for a teapot took only moments.

But it was long enough: when she got back to the room the dress had been ripped to shreds.

And now here it was hanging in tatters at Gabrielle's.

Kyra had always assumed it had been thrown out. Yet Ariana must have brought it here thinking it could be salvaged. Or looking to hide the evidence of her tantrum. Kyra lifted one of the torn bits of silk hanging off the dress and drew a line with the same needle coated in Melt elixir that she'd used on the door. The tightly woven fibers relaxed their grip and unraveled, and the strip of fabric came away.

Destroying the dress? That was just Ariana being Ariana. A tantrum.

No, what had bothered Kyra was what happened in the days that followed. Ariana *changed*. She'd thrown herself into the wedding preparations and avoided Kyra, refusing to talk to her. Eventually, she banished Kyra from her company altogether.

And then, a few weeks later, Kyra was brought to her knees by the second vision she'd ever had in her life.

The princess stood at the top of the castle parapet— newly married, in a hideous pink wedding gown. As she raised her arms, the gown turned a deep burnt charcoal, all of the frills burning off and crumpling to the ground, her blue eyes changing to deepest black. The darkness that was coiled inside of her spread out, cloaking the land in night.

Evergreen trees withered and died, flowers melted, grapes fell from the vine, and a blackness shrouded the buildings of the city so thickly that they cracked under the weight. And then the vision jumbled and leaped ahead to a bleak future: Prison cells filled to bursting, slaves in chains at the Saturday market. Famine sweeping the land, wars raging, and the rivers swelling with the blood of the dying.

Color had left the Kingdom of Mohr, and with it all hope and beauty.

Through the Nuptial Bond—the magical connection that bound Ariana to the land on her wedding day—she would poison the kingdom.

That was why Kyra had to kill her before her wedding.

Sixteen

As Kyra made her way to get Rosie from Fred's hotel through the dark, winding, crowded streets of Wexford, she eavesdropped on the people around her.

They talked nonstop in the way of folks who've had too much drink. There were mean jibes about a huge band of magic-working Gypsies who'd been driven out of the city— "Gypsy rabble," one man called them—and gossip that the Princess Killer was hiding somewhere in the city. "They're going to turn out every bed in the city to find that murderous scamp!" a woman brayed. And everywhere was talk of the wedding—how it was going to be the biggest celebration the kingdom had seen in decades. "Something so grand it'll make this festival look like a sparkler on a cupcake."

So intent was Kyra on listening to the crowd that she wasn't aware of the Cherry Blossom Princess processional until it was right behind her.

Kyra and everyone else were pushed up against the sides of the street to let the parade pass. They watched in awe.

The floats were beautiful and represented different elements of the holiday—from a giant mock springberry pie, to a bonfire made of shiny colored paper, to a straw-stuffed body that represented the dead King of Winter. The parade-goers held their torches high, flickering light dancing across their faces. Last of all was the Cherry Blossom Princess, with her guard of local boys dressed in solemn uniforms, and the local girl herself all decked out in over-the-top finery like a blossom of springtime.

As Kyra watched them go by, she caught sight of Dartagn just across the road from her. Next to him, like a loyal dog, was Hal. They were talking.

Then Hal's head came up. And looked right at Kyra.

He stared for a moment, then went back to his discussion with Dartagn.

Kyra's heart pounded. *I'm wearing a glamour, I'm wearing a glamour, I'm wearing a glamour.*

But she wasn't going to take any risks. While the captain and Hal were looking away, she joined the parade. She grabbed a torch from an older, plump man. Shock crossed his face, but then he shrugged. The uniformed float-handler beside him nodded to her as she lifted the torch.

At the first alley entrance, Kyra thrust the torch back into the plump man's hands and elbowed her way through the line of parade watchers. She took the most direct route she could to Fred's inn.

Once inside the Thorny Rose, Kyra used Release powder on the door to Fred's room. She'd expected to find him gone but was still relieved the room was empty.

Or nearly so. There on a pillow was the tiny pink pig, all curled up.

Rosie.

Something inside Kyra lit up at the sight of her. She tried to push the feeling away, but it engulfed her and made her eyes sting with unshed tears.

She'd missed the little pig.

Kyra scooped up the sleeping Rosie, anxious to leave as quickly as possible. The room bore signs of Fred everywhere—there was a wedge of cheese sitting out, half the loaf of bread she'd seen him buy earlier, the olive oil from the night of the campfire.

Bad enough that she'd gone all soft at the sight of a pig. Now Kyra's feelings were threatening to overwhelm her because of a few stupid campfire memories, a ghost of a kiss in the night, and the sensation of invisible arms around her in the soft, misty rain.

It was all more than she could handle. She needed to get out of there.

Something else about the room bothered her too—something intimate about being in Fred's space when he wasn't there. Even if it was only a hotel room. She felt like she was violating his trust—taking more away with her than just the pig.

Kyra quickly locked the door and made her way down the hall to the back stairs.

The piece of silk from Ariana's ruined wedding dress rested in Kyra's pocket. She'd wait until Rosie woke up to pin it into her basket.

Outside, she slipped through the back gate of the inn, and turned south to avoid the crowds.

And came face-to-face with Hal. Dressed impeccably, as usual, his long rich velvet cloak swirling around him as he moved to block her way.

Her ex-fiancé must have seen her go into the hotel and had been waiting for her. It was only then Kyra realized that her glamour had started to wear off. If one was looking closely, as it was evident Hal had been, you could see both layers—the glamour and the reality of Kyra beneath it. She cursed her own carelessness and palmed a throwing needle with her free hand.

Except, the first words out of Hal's mouth were so unexpected that Kyra paused.

"You've got the necklace," he said.

The necklace had fallen out of the front of her shirt when Kyra had leaned down to scoop up Rosie. "I do. Why, is the floozy who you meant it for missing it?"

Hal looked hurt, his handsome face wrinkling. "Kyra, I bought it for you."

Before Kyra could think of a response, Hal quickly moved, and Kyra looked down to discover the tip of a green-glowing poisoned sword at her throat.

"But that was before you became a criminal, my dear.

I'm afraid, Kyra, that I can no longer offer you my hand in marriage."

"*I know,*" Kyra said, exasperated. "I'm the one who left you. *First.*"

"I bought the necklace after you moved back to Wexford," Hal said, ignoring her, the tip of his sword never wavering from her throat. "There was a new stall at the Saturday market, and I thought, maybe . . ." He reached out as though to touch the cord around her neck with his free hand, but stopped himself. "I was hoping we could get back together again." He shook his head. "Before I learned who you really are. Now look at you. Stealing a pig. You've turned into a common thief."

"Hal, this is my property." Kyra gestured to the sleeping pig with her chin. "I'm just collecting it."

Hal looked her in the eye. "I know why you tried to kill her, Kyra."

Kyra stared at him, stunned. "You do?" How could he understand? Had she misjudged him?

"Of course." He ran his free hand through his hair. "You were jealous."

"*Jealous.*" Kyra stamped down the fury that threatened to bubble to the surface. The sword was so close to her neck, even a small movement could prick her and send its poison coursing through her body.

"Of me and Ariana."

"*What?*"

"It makes sense when you look at the events." He counted off on the fingers of his free hand. "One, she and I danced

together by candlelight at the Imbolc Festival, which, by the way, everyone does—it didn't mean anything! Two, you and I fought. Three, right after that, you moved out. And four, a couple weeks later, you're throwing a poison dart at Ariana."

Kyra couldn't believe it. She and Hal had fought because Kyra had been worried about the princess—Ari hadn't been herself since slashing her wedding dress. It was beyond strange that the princess was suddenly the life of the party—even dancing with Hal, whom she normally detested.

He cocked his head. "And you missed. I didn't know you EVER missed."

Kyra glared at him. "I'm aware of that." The throwing needle she had been about to use moments before was dangling loosely in her hand. "The idea that I would murder my best friend because I was jealous is insane, Hal. Why would I be jealous? Ariana only put up with you because of me. I assured her that even though you sometimes seemed a bit stupid, you were really a brilliant potioner. But now I see that being a brilliant potioner has absolutely nothing to do with whether or not you're an idiot. Somehow you manage both."

For a brief moment, Hal looked wounded. "We'll see if the princess thinks I'm an idiot now that I've caught you."

"Think so?" Kyra darted the Doze-tipped needle underhanded into Hal's leg, quickly pulling back from his sword as he went down.

Still holding Rosie with one arm, Kyra bent over his sleeping body for the second time in a week. "My putting you to sleep is getting to be a habit," she muttered. She felt a twinge of regret. He *was* heartbreakingly handsome. And they'd shared a lot. She considered leaving behind the necklace. It didn't seem right to take it.

But its nighttime glow was too useful.

Kyra felt someone approaching from behind. Turning, she quickly smacked her thighs and blew sleeping potion at the person.

Ned's round face. Her other ex-colleague sank into unconsciousness.

But not before he'd touched her shoulder.

She looked down and realized what he'd done as the mark glowed briefly red before fading to nothing.

He knew her reflexes, knew she'd turn as quickly as she had, and he'd had the foresight to reach out to touch her even as she was knocking him out.

She was tagged.

Seventeen

Kyra sprinted through the darkened forest at an all-out run.

She ran and ran and kept running, Rosie jostling in her arms, trying to put as much distance between herself and her pursuers as she could. She ran until tears were streaming down her face and her breath was coming in gasps.

This was nothing like being hunted before—it was a million times worse. They'd know exactly where she was. It would just be a matter of getting to her.

Her only hope now was that a big enough head start would make a difference.

Of course, they'd be able to travel twice as quickly on horseback as she could on foot.

Nothing could stop a potions tag. It could be confused by cloaking it in other magic, or by hiding amid a huge crowd of people, but that didn't stop the tag; it only put it off the track for a moment. Eventually the tracker would be able to find his prey again.

The taggee never felt a thing, but the hand of the tracker would grow warmer and warmer the closer he got to his prey. By the time he found the tagged person, his hand would be burning and he'd do anything to touch the object of his hunt. That was the only thing that could stop a tag—direct, deliberate contact of the tracker with his marked quarry.

And maybe even worse, Kyra thought, was that Hal had just tried to *break up* with her. Like she hadn't already cut things off before she'd moved back to Wexford!

Clearly Ariana had been right about him all along.

It had started the previous summer. She and Hal had been working on a new cloaking potion, a vast improvement on the potion Kyra and Ariana had used to sneak out of the castle. Ned had fallen asleep at his worktable by the window, his mouth open, an occasional snore rumbling out.

"This is it." Kyra had let the last drop of the red elixir she was holding fall into the vial in front of them. She could feel Hal's breathless reaction beside her as the liquid changed from muddy brown to transparent.

"Kyra," he said. "I think we've done it." He gently swirled the bottle around, then put little test drops on the ink-dipped pen in front of them.

The pen vanished.

Kyra dropped her head closer to the table. The air around where the pen should be shimmered a bit, but way down at one on the visibility scale. Negligible.

There was no sign of the pen itself. You'd never know it was there.

Kyra let out a little yelp of excitement and was swept up in Hal's arms. He swung her around, then set her on her feet.

"We," he said, "are brilliant." Then he leaned forward and kissed her smack on the mouth.

A friendly gesture in a moment of heightened excitement. *Except . . .*

"Kyra," he'd said. "I love you."

"That's sweet, Hal." Kyra reached up to pinch his cheek. "I love you too."

"No, not as a friend. I *really* love you, Kyra. Working here beside you these past months, I've never been happier. I think we should get married."

Kyra had almost fallen off her lab stool.

It had taken him months to convince her, and when she'd said yes—shortly before her sixteenth birthday and the silly underwear gift from Ariana—she'd thought she was sure. It was the right thing to do, wasn't it? And working well with someone, doing something you cared about—that was more or less love, wasn't it?

Kyra tried to push away the memory of that moment. She knew now that she wasn't in love with Hal, not by a long shot, but she missed the easy companionship she'd had with him and Ned. She'd been happy. And now—

If they caught her, the least that could happen would be imprisonment.

More likely she'd hang.

As the sun sank beneath the trees, Kyra saw a sparkle of water up ahead. She stopped and set Rosie and her pack beneath a tree, then got out her waterskins.

The bank down to the water was carpeted in browned pine needles, and their sharp scent revived Kyra, who felt like she almost couldn't take one more step. She was tired and forlorn. No closer to the princess than she was three months ago. And now she was tagged. Things couldn't get any worse for her.

At the edge of the stream she reached down to fill the first skin, the water icy over her hands. She watched the reflection of the trees on the water, the small yellow leaves twirling in the eddies.

A shriek burst out from Rosie.

Kyra turned, and there was Rosie being attacked by a wild dog. The pig squealed again.

Even as Kyra leaped up, shouting, the wild dog sank its teeth into Rosie and started shaking her back and forth.

"NO!" Kyra shouted, letting the waterskin fall to the ground and throwing a needle. "Drop her!"

She hit the wild dog square on the side. It fell to the ground, its jaws releasing Rosie. She tumbled to the earth and lay absolutely still. There were bloody puncture holes where the dog's teeth had sunk into her belly.

The sight of the little wounded pig drove Kyra to her knees.

Cold fear gripped her heart, and all thoughts of her mission fled her mind.

She couldn't lose Rosie.

Kyra touched a hand to Rosie's chest. The pit-pat of a beating heart pulsed under her fingers. She tore off the hem of her shirt and wrapped it around the pig.

"Rosie, I'm so, so sorry." Why hadn't she brought a single healing potion with her? Her only friend in the entire world lay bleeding to death at her feet, and she was too exhausted to think clearly enough to come up with a way to keep Rosie alive. Kyra felt again like things could get no worse.

That's when she heard the voices behind her. "She's here. Close by." Ned.

"Spread out the troops, Sergeant." Hal's voice was so cold, so sure of himself.

"You heard him!" a harsh man's voice barked out. "Fan out!"

Kyra gingerly scooped up Rosie and ran as quickly and as quietly as she could in the opposite direction, tears streaming down her face, her body racked with fatigue.

It took a good long while before the voices faded. But Kyra didn't think for a moment that she'd lost them. They were right on her trail.

She didn't dare look down to see if Rosie was still with her. She convinced herself that she could feel the little pig breathing, but couldn't bring herself to check.

She'd been jogging along for hours, feeling so tired it was an effort to keep her eyes on the trail and her legs moving, when the trail ended in the shallows of a wicked-looking bog. It appeared from nowhere and stretched in front of her as far as she could see, a swampy mess of fallen trees bearded with moss, and low-lying fog clinging to the water, and the stink of things decomposing in murk.

Kyra tried to pull herself up short at the marshy edge.

But she was unsteady on her feet from running for hours straight. And instead of stopping, she tripped over her own feet and tumbled directly into the mucky water.

Only it wasn't mucky water at all. The ground beneath her looked exactly like regular dirt. It *was* regular dirt.

Kyra raised herself up, keeping Rosie tucked under her arm, and looked around. As she got to her feet, she could see the bog take form in the air, coalescing out of nothingness. She felt the cold cling of the fog, smelled the stench of rotting things, heard the lapping of the swamp water. Then she ducked her head down and watched it all vanish.

The bog was an illusion.

She stumbled forward, hunched over, working her way deeper into the bog glamour, knowing the magic of it would help confuse Ned's tag.

Kyra had read about such large-scale illusions but never seen one: it took many magic workers to pull one off, and finding that many powerful people together was rare. Potioners' schools, or witches' covens, or—

Gypsies.

Kyra saw the glimmer of the caravans' lanterns before she saw any people—their wagons were ringed around a large fire. She staggered toward the nearest wagon, but it only seemed to get farther and farther away the more steps she took, until finally she fell to her knees, the lantern light an ever-distant glow.

Of course they'd have other protection spells, she thought, realizing her confusion was another ward placed by the Gypsies on the caravan.

It was her last thought before she collapsed in exhaustion.

Eighteen

A SCENT OF INCENSE and honey was floating on the air.

Mmmm . . . honey. Kyra's stomach growled in response. She was lying on her back on a soft pallet, and when she opened her eyes she was staring up at a brilliant multicolored cloth roof lit by sunshine. Images of red and gold butterflies flew among the flowers on the ceiling tapestry.

The warmth of the sun made her want to shut her eyes again and sink back into sleep. But then a thought darted into her brain and pricked her skin.

Rosie!

She sat up and looked around, but the pig was nowhere in sight.

Struggling to get out of bed, Kyra felt warm hands rest

on top of her shoulders. "It's okay," a melodious voice said. "Your little friend is fine."

Kyra turned and faced the woman who spoke. "Fine? But she was bleeding to death!"

"It's been taken care of." The old woman looked like a dragon, her skin wrinkled and scaly, her gaze glinty-eyed and wily.

"How?" Kyra asked, then knew the answer. "Potions." Her insides relaxed. "You must be a potioner."

The woman nodded. "I'm Nadya." She handed a steaming mug to Kyra, and the honey smell intensified. "Drink this, and I'll get her for you."

The liquid was warm and sweet and filled her with a delicious buzzing. Kyra felt a dull shock when she realized she was actually too worn out to work out what potions could have been put in it. She just didn't care.

The woman came around with a bundled-up Rosie. "She needs sleep after the healing she's had."

Kyra hugged the bundle close and was completely embarrassed when two tears plopped down on the sleeping pig. She brushed her eyes with one hand as Rosie snuggled in with a contented grunt. "Thank you so much. I thought I'd lost her."

The woman's amber eyes met Kyra's olive ones. "It was my pleasure."

Then, the pig clasped against her chest, Kyra fell back into a deep sleep.

Kyra woke the next morning with a feeling of panic running through her—she needed to set off again immediately.

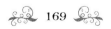

She turned over and discovered Nadya working at a table across the room, mixing up a brew that smelled of mint and lavender.

Kyra shifted Rosie in her lap and sat up, stretching her arms above her head. "Nadya, I can't thank you enough for what you've done. If there's anything I can do to repay you before we leave—"

"You aren't leaving today," the older woman said.

"But—"

"If you want your friend to heal, you will stay put. I've done what I can, but she needs more time."

Kyra looked down at the little pig in her lap: eyes shut, Rosie let out a happy huff of breath and scrunched up tighter.

Kyra couldn't leave her behind again.

"And if you, too, want to heal, you will rest. Here." Nadya gave her a mug of the minty, lavender mixture, and without even questioning what it was, Kyra drank deep.

"Nadya," Kyra said the next day, after she woke and felt fully herself for the first time in . . . days? No—*months*. "I have to leave."

"Come with me," Nadya commanded.

Kyra followed her out of the tent, Rosie napping in her arms. Around them, the encampment was alive with a quiet, happy industry. The men fixed wagons and scrubbed laundry in a nearby stream and talked, while a group of women prepared to go off into the woods to hunt berries and small game. The Gypsies' small wooden homes were all on wheels, but they were set up like a village. There was a pleasant rhythm and flow to it all, and Kyra felt as though she and Rosie had been living there for years instead of mere days. The Gypsies had been driven out of Wexford in advance of the festival, Nadya told her, and they were camping here for a spell until they figured out where to go next.

Nadya sat down across from Kyra under an enormous tree at the edge of the camp.

"You don't have to leave," she said, crossing her legs in front of her and picking some sewing out of her bag. "You could come with us when we move north. A second potioner would be a blessing."

So Nadya knew Kyra was a potioner—it was probably obvious from her potions bag. Kyra absently stroked Rosie's snout, and the pig grunted in contentment. "There's something I should tell you. There's a tracking potion on me. There are people looking for me, and if I don't leave soon, they'll find me here." The moment Hal and Ned figured out how to find her through the illusion of the bog, the whole tribe would be in danger for harboring a fugitive. The thought of the Gypsies wounded and torn away from the sun, cast into the cold and wet of the palace dungeon, sent chills through her.

Nadya didn't even look up from her stitches. "There is no tracking mark on you anymore. I took it off when we first found you."

"There's no way to remove a tracking potion, and believe me, I was tagged."

Nadya's eyes twinkled. "It's always fun to spend time with young people." She shook her head. "Always think they know everything. There are more things in this world that you don't know than you will ever imagine."

"How? Did you concoct a counter-potion?"

"No, actually, it was a bit of witchcraft."

Kyra heard herself gasp. "I thought you were a *potioner.*"

"Now, don't go getting that look of utter fear on your face—it's a very uncommon bit of witchcraft. You aren't going to find many other witches who know it, if any."

"But a witch can't—"

"I can't be both witch *and* potioner?"

"No." Kyra shook her head violently.

"Of course I can. And so can you." Nadya picked up another piece of cloth. "Just touch the spark inside of you for a moment, and you'll know that what I say is true."

Kyra couldn't help herself; she immediately tried to shut down the feeling from that place inside her—the place she'd tried to eradicate. "How did you know?"

"I'm a Seer too."

Kyra picked up the pillowcase Nadya had sewn and ran her fingers over the small perfect stitches. "What coven did you train with?"

"I didn't. Not in the way you're thinking. I spent time with a Gypsy potioner, and some more time with a Gypsy witch." Nadya set her work down and smiled at Kyra. "Look, I don't know what you're running from, and I haven't pried using my Sight. But I can offer you shelter and training,

and I wouldn't be surprised if you found yourself some companionship among the tribe, either."

Kyra made to stand up. "I can't—"

"Sit. There's no hurry to make a decision," Nadya said. "I'm not saying it's an easy life. Moving around as much as we do has its challenges, but it might be better than where you're coming from."

Kyra trembled all over. The horizon stretched out in front of her.

A new life.

But . . .

"You know what helps me make decisions?" Nadya said. "A good sweat. Nothing clears the mind like a really hot steamy sauna."

Kyra felt completely naked when, after dinner that night, she wrapped herself in nothing but a sheet and made her way across the encampment to a small caravan with smoke pouring out of the chimney. But no one gave her a second glance.

She stepped inside the sauna and was smacked by a wave of intense heat. A bench ran along one wall, a wood stove across from it. The door closed, leaving her in complete darkness. She sat on the bench and her eyes began to adjust. The stove flamed and crackled in front of her, radiating more heat than she had ever felt in her life.

Kyra had never especially liked heat, always sought shade on hot days, and never liked overheated rooms. But this was different. The steamy heat overwhelmed her, and soon an extraordinary feeling spread through her limbs. She lay down on the long bench, stretching her body out full length.

The instant her head touched the bench, she felt herself falling back—back into a memory.

It was after she'd left Hal and moved back to Wexford to be closer to Ariana. After she'd had her vision.

She was standing in front of the queen, in the throne room, her hands clutched tight behind her as she tried to think of the best way to explain what she had to say. "Your Highness, I'm worried about Ariana."

The queen quirked a razor-thin eyebrow but said nothing.

"She's not herself at all. There's something seriously wrong with her." The queen's eyes pierced Kyra. Queen Lilly, the Clear-Sighted One, seemed to look right into Kyra's soul.

"Did Ariana send you? Is this her latest scheme to get out of marriage and her duty to her country?" Obviously the queen had no idea what was going on with Ari.

"Your Highness," Kyra said, "that's just it. Ariana *doesn't* want to cancel the wedding at all. She seems to be looking forward to it—and we both know that's not her. Have you seen the new dress she's designing? It's bright pink and covered in more ruffles and bows than you'd find on all of the noblewomen's dresses put together."

The queen's response was dismissive. "Not everyone wears green to their wedding, Kyra. Pink has a long tradition. Do you object to a tribute to the Goddess of Love?"

Kyra wanted to scream. The queen was completely missing the point. Was a gaudy pink dress the sort of dress Ariana would ever wear on purpose? "It isn't just the dress. She barely acknowledges me. I'm lucky to be invited to sit in with her sewing circle. The one time I tried to talk to her alone, she pushed me away. Now she won't even look at me."

"Ariana is growing up, Kyra. I appreciate the friendship you've shown her over the years, but right now perhaps it's the ladies in her sewing circle she needs. She's about to become a married woman and take the first step to ascending the throne. The free-spirited life you lead doesn't fit who she must become right now."

Kyra stared at her.

The queen smiled unexpectedly. "She'll come back to you in the end. Just give her time. Ariana will no doubt see the value in keeping the kingdom's leading potions weapons master close to her."

See the value in keeping the kingdom's leading potions weapons master close to her? Kyra's knees trembled. The idea that their friendship would be reduced to a wise monarchical business relationship left her with an empty feeling.

The queen was wrong. Kyra knew it. But she couldn't tell her about her Sight. Kyra would have to save the kingdom—and the princess—another way.

She spent days in the library trying to find some clue as to what had happened to her friend. One by one, she ruled out every possible explanation: it wasn't a spell, a curse, the effects of a potion.

That left only the possibility of possession. The soul crushed inside the body by the weight of another.

There was no recovery from possession.

Ariana—whoever she now was—remained a threat to the kingdom. She had to be stopped.

And Kyra was going to have to be the one to do it.

She felt again the heat of the sauna and the hard bench beneath her, and for the first time in her life, embraced her spark. Her inner vision flared, this time flinging her forward. Images flooded her mind—some memories, others something more. The leering face of the witch who'd captured her and Fred. Rosie gazing up at her with trusting eyes. Her parents silently eating breakfast together. Fred, all rumpled hair and green eyes, in the garb of a king's soldier, wielding a full-length fighting staff, its sharp end glowing with a deadly poison.

And she saw the Gypsy band marching north—the apple harvest they'd find that fall, the kitten Nadya would adopt, and most of all, the empty space in the caravan where Kyra was not.

Because she wasn't going with them.

And she knew it.

Her duty lay with the Kingdom of Mohr.

Kyra felt as though she'd melted into the sauna bench. Light-headed, she got up and stepped outside, welcoming the stinging embrace of the cool spring evening.

"How was it?" Nadya asked from her perch on a bench a few feet from the door. She was whittling a small figure with her knife. "Easier to See?"

Kyra nodded grimly.

Nadya's cheeks rounded in a smile. "I thought it would be."

"But horrible," Kyra added. "Is it always like that? A big rush of random images?"

"Sometimes. With training you can direct it, to bring it out when you want to know something. But it is never an exact art." Nadya set down her knife. "This doesn't have to be a burden, but you do need to prepare yourself. The Sight will not be denied. It's only going to get stronger with each vision you have."

"I see the future," Kyra said. "It just seems so hopeless. Is it set?"

"You see *possible* futures, but that doesn't mean the future can't change. Or be changed."

"Oh." Kyra sat down on the wagon steps. "I hope you get the kitten anyway. I think it will be good for you."

"A kitten?" Nadya's voice filled with pleasure. "Let's hope that's one of your more accurate visions." She laughed, then grew serious. "When you first came, I had a vision of you. My Sight showed me the potioners' tag on you, of course, but there was more."

Kyra hugged herself in a sudden chill breeze. "What was it?"

"Your life was hanging in the balance—sometimes you fell one way, sometimes another." Nadya watched Kyra for a moment. "Either way resulted in your death. Is your mission so important that you'll throw your life away?"

Kyra swallowed. "It is."

Nadya nodded. "Then I wish you all the luck in the world." She put down her whittling and walked away.

Kyra picked up the piece of carved wood—it was the figure of a tiny pig, a basket slung below its snout, a smile on its face. She grinned and clutched it in her fist.

A little extra luck definitely couldn't hurt.

Nineteen

THE NEXT DAY, Kyra pinned the scrap of green silk into Rosie's basket, attached her leash, wrapped up some food Nadya had given her, and hefted her pack onto her shoulders. It seemed like every member of the tribe came to hug her good-bye.

Nadya gave her one last squeeze. "Be careful, my dear. The world needs you."

Kyra hugged her back. "Thank you for everything," she said, then marched off toward the wavery line on the horizon that marked the border of the bog illusion.

She took a moment to get her bearings, then set the pig down on the ground.

Immediately, Rosie strained at the leash. It looked as though she was pointing right back toward Wexford.

 179

Why was Kyra even surprised? It seemed like her whole life revolved around that city.

She took her time getting back to the capital. She kept their gait slow and made Rosie take frequent rest breaks. Their plodding pace gave her plenty of time to wonder what her vision of Fred had meant. There were lots of reasons why he might be dressed like that, why he'd have a staff.

Since her vision in the sauna, the cracks in the wall she'd built around her witch's spark had grown. As she'd hugged each of the Gypsies good-bye, images had flickered through her vision. But try as she might, she could not make her Sight do what she wanted.

She couldn't focus it on Fred.

As Kyra approached the road to Wexford, she put on the glamour of a middle-aged housewife, complete with an apron. Now she just had to hide Rosie. Hal would have spread word that the Princess Killer had a pig.

"Rosie. You're going to have to hide in my pack. Do you think you can do that?"

Rosie oinked and nudged Kyra with her snout.

Kyra gave her a carrot from the provisions Nadya had given her, tucked the rest in her apron pocket, then picked Rosie up and set her inside atop her things. The pig curled up and sighed.

"You really are a sweetheart." Kyra loosely fastened the top flap, then hefted the pack onto her back.

Traffic on the road moved slower than the last time she'd entered the city. Up ahead, Kyra could see that there were King's soldiers everywhere, watching the crowd, occasionally stopping people and questioning them—looking for the Princess Killer. Her pulse beat hard in her veins as she drew closer.

"Hey, you there!" A soldier stepped in front of Kyra.

Kyra stopped and tried to smile. "Yes?"

"Where are you coming from?"

"Littleton."

"Littleton's not far. Why do you have such a big pack?" The soldier's voice was harsh.

"I'm just bringing my cousin some country produce. She loves the roots that grow wild near my house." She dug a couple of carrots out of her apron pocket.

His eyes glazed over with boredom. "Carry on."

Kyra let out a breath and passed into the city.

She went first to the small weekday market to gather supplies. Nadya had said her Sight would grow stronger with use, so she decided to test it out. As she stepped between the open-air stalls, she mentally touched the spark within her mind. Visions bombarded her. Not just of the future, but of people's pasts as well.

She flashed on the old gentleman at the greens counter as a young boy digging in a dirt pile for worms. The little girl at the cheese stand, on the other hand, she saw as an old wrinkled woman on her deathbed. In the bakery, when Kyra went to pay for the bags of dough she'd selected, she almost said, "Congratulations" to the young woman behind the counter. She stopped herself just in time, realizing that just as surely as she knew the woman was pregnant, it was a joyful surprise the woman had yet to discover for herself.

 181

From there she went directly to Fred's inn. She paused outside his door, her cloth bag of purchases dangling from her arm. She didn't hear anything.

Kyra knocked and, when no one answered, she broke into his room.

Fred's room was, thankfully, Fredless.

His bottle of olive oil was still on the counter in the small kitchen area. Perfect. He was out, but he was still staying here.

Kyra got to work, stoking the stove with kindling she found in a bin and rummaging through cabinets and drawers. They were filled with an odd assortment of pots and pans. Glimpses of people who'd used the cookware flickered through her mind's eye as she touched each item, and she practiced pushing each vision to the back of her mind so that she could focus on her work.

By the time Fred bounded through the door with Langley that evening, Kyra's housewife glamour had worn off, and the stage was set.

"Kitty?" He dropped his day pack on the chair by the door.

She'd thought she was ready for him, but his face still took her breath away. He wasn't handsome the way Hal was—Hal was too perfect, too long-lashed, too well-coifed. Fred was beautiful in a completely different, effortless way. His green-gold eyes sent a shiver of happiness down to Kyra's very core.

Kyra recovered herself. "Thought I'd surprise you!" She threw off the apron she'd borrowed to replace the one that had vanished when her glamour wore off. Underneath it was a floaty white blouse. Kyra never thought she'd feel this way, but it felt nice to wear something soft and light and pretty after months in the same black durable shirt. She looked good.

"Fred, I'm so sorry I stole Rosie away." She watched to see if he'd heard of the Princess Killer by now. But his face remained blandly happy and impassive.

He sat on a chair at the tiny table and leaned back, his legs out in front of him. "She was your pig. You weren't really stealing her." Langley rubbed noses with Rosie.

"You were right—she didn't belong with a family, and I shouldn't have given her to them. I realized that I couldn't live without her, so I stole her back. Anyway, I made you dinner to repay you for all your kindnesses to me."

"Something does smell good. . . ." Fred reached down to pet Rosie, who had come over and was anxiously butting her head against his leg and looking up at him with shameless adoration. She settled at his feet. Then Fred stretched his arms overhead, and Kyra caught a glimpse of his flat stomach as his shirt lifted slightly.

She blinked rapidly. *That* was distracting. "You're going to love it."

The room seemed really quite small. Kyra tried to focus her witch's Sight for a moment to see if it would tell her anything about the mysterious man in front of her. Nothing so much as flickered in her vision. What good was this power if she couldn't control it?

She turned to the counter and began cutting slices of the steaming-hot strudel she'd cooked—layers of fresh spring

spinach and salty cheese wrapped in a light flaky dough.

Fred came up behind her, his hand gentle on her back as he leaned over her shoulder to look at what she'd made. "Wow. That looks delicious."

Kyra caught the scent of him, all spicy and woodsy, and had to keep herself from burying her face in his hair. Then he leaned over and landed a tiny kiss on her cheek, below her left eye, sending a spark right down to her toes.

It was only a kiss. A tiny little butterfly kiss. Kyra could handle that.

She loaded up two plates with strudel and mounds of fresh-herb-and-tangy-olive salad while Fred spread a blanket on the floor between the bed and the table. "Table's too small for two."

Kyra brought the plates over and gingerly set one down in front of Fred and another across from him.

Then, settled on the floor with the animals beside them, they ate.

Kyra was in a tiny pocket of goodness that she wanted to savor before it was gone.

She enjoyed every last morsel of the meal she'd made. Fred was strangely quiet, offering compliments to her cooking, but mostly focusing on the food in front of him. "It's *good*," he said, more than once.

Then it was time for dessert.

Kyra was really proud of it. She put a heaping plateful in front of Fred. "Homemade springberry pie."

He smiled at her, his fork poised in his hand. "You really didn't have to do all this, Kitty. But I'm glad you did."

"Eat up!" Kyra gestured with the pie knife.

He took a big bite. "Come sit next to me." Fred patted the blanket beside him, and Kyra scootched over. He put his free arm around her.

He took another bite. Two. "You're a great cook. Your talents are wasted on the dairy industry."

He ate a couple forkfuls more, then swallowed and set down his silverware. He leaned toward her and pressed his lips against hers.

Her whole body reacted. She melted into him and began kissing him back, wishing that things weren't the way they were.

Fred went still, and she pulled away.

He slumped down to the floor, eyes closed.

Kyra scooped a nibble off her own plate. It really *was* a delicious pie. The berries were deliciously tart against the sweet crust.

Perfect for hiding a sleeping potion.

Kyra kept her fingers crossed that he'd had enough. She eyed his plate critically. He'd only had a half dozen bites. But that should provide her with enough time to find the princess without Fred "accidentally" interfering—whoever he really was. She didn't trust how he kept "accidentally" crossing her path. Now she could be sure it wouldn't happen again. Before he woke, she'd be far enough away that he couldn't follow.

His body's natural nighttime sleep cycle would probably

kick in where the potion left off, and he'd think he'd eaten too much and fallen asleep.

Kyra laid him on his back, propping up his head with a pillow. His hair was soft in her hands as she arranged his head so he would be able breathe freely.

Before she could think about what she was doing, she leaned forward and dropped a small kiss just above his left eyebrow. He did smell wonderful.

She gathered her pack, making sure her potions pouch was safely tucked inside, and took one last look. Completely relaxed, his face looked ready to break into a smile at any moment.

Langley lay down beside Fred, his big dog head resting on his front paws.

"Keep an eye on him, okay?" Kyra said.

Kyra's glamour was gone, but it was late enough that she hoped the shadows outside would be disguise enough. The festival was long over and people rarely came out this late at night. The streets were quiet as she followed Rosie on her hunt. The little pig walked right up to the front door of Gabrielle's Fine Dresses and sat, looking up at Kyra expectantly.

"No, Rosie. I know this is where the cloth came from, but I'm trying to find the person it belonged to originally. Come on, girl. I know you can do this."

But Rosie was unyielding. She began scraping the door with her hooves.

Kyra gave up, brought Rosie around to the side door, and

 186

broke into the shop. Maybe she'd find something interesting in Ari's closet that she hadn't seen before. Something besides the wedding dress Ari had ruined. Or maybe Rosie, who was headed right for the curtain concealing the private closets, needed to come into contact with the whole dress before turning around and tracking down the princess.

Except Rosie didn't lead her to the closet.

She wound her way through the reams of multicolored fabric on display in the main room of the shop and through the curtain to where the closet was located. But instead of stopping there, she headed for the half-open storeroom door and pushed her way through with her snout.

Kyra followed and watched as Rosie scrambled her way to the top of the slippery pile of mannequins and began digging through them.

Finally, about halfway down the stack, she settled herself on top of one of them with a satisfied grunt.

"Come on, Rosie. Those things give me the creeps. Let's go check out Ari's closet." The mannequins' frozen, painted eyes seemed to stare at Kyra.

Rosie just snorted.

"Rosie, come here!"

Rosie stayed where she was, not so much as lifting her head at Kyra's voice.

Kyra stepped into the room, wishing that Rosie would just come when she was called. If it had been daylight and the shop bustling with costumers, maybe this stack of naked wooden bodies wouldn't seem so creepy. But here in the silence with only the faint glow of Kyra's necklace lighting the room, there was something unnerving about the flat, sightless dolls' eyes watching her.

She made her way to Rosie and reached down to scoop her up. Just as her hands touched the little pig, she caught sight of the mannequin Rosie was on top of.

And almost screamed.

It looked just like Ariana.

Twenty

CREEPY.

Kyra clutched Rosie to her chest, staring in awe at the blond-haired mannequin in front of her. It was uncanny how much this stiff, dead thing looked like the princess. It even had her frizzy hair. Maybe Gabrielle's tailors did their work for the princess on a life-size model of her, just to be certain they got everything *just* right. Maybe.

Kyra set Rosie down on the floor and watched in dismay as the pig scrambled back up on top of the mannequin. Weird.

She went back into the other room and took down a lantern hanging on a hook, lit the wick, and brought it into the storeroom with her. She knelt by the mannequin that looked like her friend. It was perfect. It even had the mole on her belly that Ariana said was shaped like a teddy bear.

Except *this* Ariana was carved out of wood.

And had a tiny and very contented-looking pig curled up on its stomach.

Was Rosie wrong to lead Kyra here, to this thing? Or was there more to this mannequin, a lie in its appearance?

Kyra took out her potions bag and picked through the bottles.

Her fingers closed on the potion she'd spent so much time and energy acquiring. The potion she'd risked breaking into the Master Trio's flat for and had ended up finding on the floor across the hall, in Ellie the hermit's living room.

Official name—Peccant Pentothal; *potion number*—07 211; *previous working name*—Red Skull Serum.

The potion she'd used on Arlo at the king's bidding.

The potion that had nearly killed him. Which, diluted with pine oil, had transformed him into wood. Arlo had been told of Kyra's mistake; maybe he'd repeated it on someone else.

Kyra took several deep breaths to still her hands before beginning a far different dilution process for the Red Skull Serum. The *proper* dilution.

Properly prepared, the serum could reveal any falsehood—including magical ones. *Could it counteract this spell?*

Improperly prepared—well, depending on the potions used on this painted doll, it could end up destroying the mannequin, the storeroom, and anyone in it.

Kyra glanced down, patted the piglet's head, and scooped

her up. "You're going to wait outside," she told Rosie, setting her in the main showroom and closing the door on her.

She unscrewed the top of an empty dropper bottle and filled it with dilution fluid. Carefully, she went through the many steps of the process, repeating them to herself as she worked through every possible counter-reaction, just to make certain she wasn't overlooking anything. She put the cap back on the dropper bottle and swirled the contents around inside.

As she worked, questions ran wild through her head. *What if Ariana came to the shop to get her wedding dress mended and never left? What if I don't have to kill my best friend after all?*

She uncapped the bottle and sucked a tiny bit of the serum up into the dropper.

Her hand hovered over the mannequin. It stared at her with its painted blue eyes so much like Ariana's, blond hair in a pouf around its face. It didn't have the identical features as the models lying around it, and it was thicker and sturdier.

This has to be her.

Kyra squeezed one drop of diluted serum on the wooden lips. A small bead of moisture stood out—the wetness turning the pink paint a shade darker where it lay.

Nothing happened.

Kyra went back over her calculations. She didn't believe she'd made it too strong; she'd taken every care to make sure it wasn't lethal. Had it not been strong enough? Or had she completely lost her mind and this was just what it appeared to be—a replica of the kingdom's princess?

A series of images clicked together in her head: Arlo going rigid when she'd administered the wrong mix of the serum to him. The vial of Peccant Pentothal she'd found in Ellie's lodgings. The way Rosie had first led her to Ellie, who was somehow mixed up in the princess's disappearance.

But even if this mannequin *were* Ariana, it wasn't flesh and blood: it was a wooden figure. It could no more drink a drop of serum than Kyra could cough out a splinter of wood.

And it was all her fault. It was *her* poison that had been used on Ariana. Kyra had failed in her mission to kill whatever had taken Ariana's place, just like she had failed to rescue the princess from this horrible fate.

After everything else she'd suffered, this was just too much: Kyra wept.

She hugged the stiff figure and sobbed loudly, her tears slicking her cheeks and the hard face of the Ariana mannequin, crying out, "I'm sorry, Ari—so sorry. It's my fault." She cried until she'd dampened the doll's wooden visage, cried until she didn't have any more tears. She ignored the scratching of the pig at the door and just held on to her friend.

Then something absolutely miraculous happened. Beneath her arms, the wooden stiffness warmed and began to soften. Kyra pulled back and looked at the mannequin. The painted skin brightened into flesh, and a sparkling blue replaced the dull paint of the eyes.

Kyra barked out a laugh and dragged her hand across her snotty nose.

Her tears! She hadn't diluted the solution enough, after all—she'd overlooked the necessary admixture of salt water as an alkaline. Kyra laughed again and shook the figure in her arms.

Ariana sucked in a great gulp of breath.

Then she turned those sparkling blue eyes on Kyra. And coughed in her face.

"Kitty, I feel *awful*." Her eyes spun as she looked around the room, then she rolled over onto her side and wheezed. "Ugh. And why aren't I wearing any clothes?"

Kyra smiled. "It's a long story."

Twenty-one

For a long while, Ariana couldn't move her body much, though she had little trouble moving her jaw. She talked nonstop.

"Why is there a *pig* trying to climb on top of me?" she'd asked after Kyra let Rosie back into the room. The little pig kept butting Ariana with her head until Kyra reached down and popped the small scrap of green silk out of her basket. "By the Goddess, Kitty, I'm completely *naked*!" she'd complained, until Kyra found her a simple day dress in the old Choizie Laurent closet. And "I am *so* glad to see you," she said as she, at last, started stretching out the kinks in her long limbs.

Kyra grabbed up her friend in a huge hug, and Ariana hugged her back—so hard that Kyra's tears threatened to spill all over again.

There was no doubt that this was the real Ariana. Kyra didn't need her Sight to tell her that. "That pig is named Rosie, by the way, and she helped me find you. You should be nice to her."

The little pig sank down onto her haunches next to Ariana, closed her eyes, and gave out a great big gusty sigh, as though she needed a nap after her exertions.

"Did you really try to kill me? And missed? *You?*" Ariana asked, drawing the day dress down over her torso.

At Kyra's confused look, she added, "I was frozen, but I wasn't deaf. The only thing I could do was eavesdrop. Being a clotheshorse is *so* boring."

"Um, yeah. Tried to kill you. And missed," Kyra said, settling on the floor and petting Rosie. "But obviously it wasn't *really* you—you were here." The giddiness Kyra was feeling swelled into an all-encompassing joy as the thought truly struck home—she wasn't going to have to kill her best friend.

"And you knew that it wasn't really me?" Ariana gently pulled on her elbow with her other hand, stretching her shoulder blade and the muscles in her back.

"Well, no, not exactly."

Ariana eyed her over her elbow.

"Actually . . . I thought you were possessed."

Ariana looked at her thoughtfully. "There's no cure for possession."

"None." Kyra squeezed her hands together. "You have no idea how glad I am that I was wrong!"

"Still, Kyra—killing me? That's a little harsh."

Kyra was going to have to tell Ari about her vision. She would never forget the look on her friend's face the day they'd met, when Ari had told Kyra that witches weren't even human. Ari didn't know about Kyra's witch spark, and she wished things could stay that way. The last thing Kyra needed was to lose her best friend when she'd only just gotten her back.

"Don't give me that look. Did I, or did I not, just save your life?"

"You did." Ariana reached out and squeezed Kyra's shoulder. "Thank you."

"No problem." Kyra felt the weight of the last three months lift off of her as she leaned against her friend. "So, what happened, Ariana?"

Ariana shrugged in response and put on the long soft pantaloons she wore under her dresses to give her more mobility. "I came down here with my ripped-up wedding gown. I was horrified about what I'd done and thought maybe Gabrielle could fix it and hide the evidence. When I came into the shop, the girl at the counter directed me to the back room. The moment I walked in, I was frozen."

"A witch's sticky trap," Kyra said.

"If you say so." Ariana shrugged. "All I heard was a man's voice—an old man. 'Oh, foo!' he said. I felt a drop of potion on my hand, and then my body went all—well, you saw what I looked like." She shuddered. "Whoever it was dragged me into this storeroom, cut my clothes off me, and stacked me with the rest of the dummies."

"And sent a fake princess back to the palace to take your place."

"Do we have to get rid of the fake princess? If she wants my life, she can have it. She can marry the prince, run the kingdom, and end up shut inside that palace."

"The fake princess is evil, Ariana. She's going to destroy the kingdom." Kyra could feel her heart pounding, and the room began spinning around her. She'd thought for a moment that she'd be able to somehow avoid this.

But she needed to convince Ariana completely.

The kingdom needed her.

"And I know she's evil," Kyra said, her olive eyes meeting Ariana's blue ones, "because I'm a witch."

"You're my best friend—I'd know if you were a witch."

"I had a vision of the fake princess destroying the kingdom." Kyra shut her eyes. "That's my power as a witch—I'm a Seer."

"A Seer?"

Kyra opened her mouth to explain, when the door burst open.

Fred flew into the room, Langley beside him. He caught sight of Kyra and Ariana sitting together on the floor and shouted, "Stop! I can't let you do this, Kyra!"

Langley came over to Kyra and put his nose in her palm.

"Fred?" Kyra rubbed the pup's snout. "You're supposed to be sleeping."

Fred stood blinking, as though he wasn't quite sure what he was seeing. His clothes were disheveled from his nap on the floor, and he had a spot of springberry pie on his chin. "I dozed off for a minute or two, and by the time I was awake, you were gone."

Darn. He hadn't eaten enough pie. "And how in the world did you find me here?"

"Oh. I, um, nicked your tracking potion earlier and tagged you while you were cutting the strudel. I had a feeling I might not be seeing you again unless I took matters into my own hands. Speaking of which—"

Fred walked over and touched her gently on the shoulder. "That stuff burns."

"You've got pie on your chin."

He swiped at his jaw with the back of his hand.

Kyra realized that Ariana was glaring at her.

"What are you doing with *him*?" the princess demanded.

"Fred? I'm not doing anything with him. How do you know Fred?" As Kyra was saying this, something struck her: he'd called her Kyra. Not only did Ariana know who Fred was, Fred knew who Kyra was too.

"Hmmm . . . let's see." Ariana tapped her chin like she was thinking. "Well, there was that whole marriage thing that was supposed to happen."

"What?"

Stiffly, Ariana stood and walked through to the Choizie Laurent closet. Reaching deep inside, she pulled something from the highest shelf and brought it over: a small portrait.

Of Fred. With the words HIS ROYAL HIGHNESS, PRINCE FREDERICK LANTANA III, OF ARCADIA.

Kyra felt like she'd been thrown down from a tall height.

Fred—who, less than an hour ago had been kissing her—was engaged to her best friend.

He'd mentioned his dad was a perfumer. Of course the king of Arcadia would be a perfumer. Arcadia was famous for its perfumeries.

Fred eyed her uneasily. "Can we discuss the whole assassination thing? Are you planning to murder the princess any time soon?"

Kyra and Ariana simultaneously rolled their eyes.

"Not at the moment," Kyra said. "Though, there's *another* royal in the room I'd like to see dead."

"Oh, that's good. Really good! We're clearly starting off on the right path here." He sat down on a giant bolt of purple fabric. Langley had found Rosie and curled himself around her.

"Ugh," Ariana said. "He's even worse in person." She smiled innocently at him and shrugged. "Sorry 'bout that, I can't help it—Kyra gave me a truth serum!"

"Right." He smiled nervously. "I'm sorry that I lied to you, Kyra. I can't say that I wasn't out looking for the princess's assassin. I was."

"So it wasn't just coincidence that I ran into you."

"Actually, it was. I wasn't exactly aggressive in my search for the assassin." He shifted his weight. "More like, if I happened to run into her and captured her, that would be okay.

I never expected to find the assassin crossing a stream in her underwear with a pig on top of her head."

A puff of laughter escaped Ariana.

"I never dreamed the assassin was you."

Kyra and Ariana exchanged a look.

"God's honest. The confusion potion at the witch's should have been a clue, but I was so sure I knew who you were: Kitty, the dairymaid with the pig."

Ariana interrupted. "Wait, you said you were a dairymaid?" She started cackling. "Oh, Kitty, you are the best. Why in the world would anyone believe *you* were a dairymaid?"

Fred pushed his hands through his rumpled hair. "I only knew for sure it was you when I saw that poison in your bag. That's the truth. Do you want to give me some of this truth serum I keep hearing so much about?"

Kyra shook her head.

"I didn't know what I was going to do, but I couldn't let you go. I had to figure something out."

"Well, you did a great job," Kyra said. "You only lost me completely for the better half of a week."

"You are a slippery kitty cat," Ariana said. "I'll give him that. A half week's not too bad, really."

"So," Fred said, "you aren't trying to kill the princess anymore?"

"Oh, I'm still trying to kill the princess, just not this one."

Kyra let Ariana explain everything to Fred, figuring she should have plenty of energy for storytelling—she hadn't been on the hunt for the past three months. Right now, several

months of vacation on the floor of a tailor's shop sounded kind of nice to Kyra.

Her heart hurt.

She'd found Ariana, but she'd lost so much—her career, her friendship with Ned and Hal, and now Fred, who was smiling dopily at the princess as she talked. His fiancée.

Kyra's heart was breaking.

Ariana nudged her. "What do you think, Kitty? Is the impostor princess a shape-shifter?"

Kyra stamped down the feelings that were threatening to engulf her. "She doesn't have any of the traits of the shape-shifters in the books at the palace library. Maybe—"

The front door of the shop banged open, and in strode an old man.

"Oh, foo!" the old man shouted when he saw the unfrozen Ariana. "What are you—"

Recognition lit Ariana's face. "You!"

Recognition lit the old man's face too, as he saw Kyra. "You!"

And Kyra sighed and said, *"You."*

Because the old man was Ellie the hermit.

Twenty-two

KYRA HAD GUESSED AS MUCH, but now she knew for sure: Ellie was the kidnapper.

It was Ellie who'd frozen Ariana in this back room, Ellie who'd stacked her up with the mannequins, Ellie who'd gotten rid of the princess's things. That's why he'd had Kyra's poison in his apartment, that's why Ariana recognized him, and that's why Rosie had first led Kyra to him. That bit of scarf had probably been in Ellie's keeping for so long that he'd stunk it up with his old-man smell before it ended up in Arlo's possession.

But why had Ellie kidnapped Ariana?

Kyra slipped a clean needle out of her holster and hid it behind her back. Taking him out with a Doze dart would stop him from escaping, but it wouldn't help her find out what she wanted to know.

"Ellie," Kyra said, "so nice of you to drop in. What brings you here at this time of night? Or anywhere, really—since you so rarely leave Newman House?"

"My own business here, isn't it?" Ellie said. "I own this place, can come around here any time I want."

Ariana and Kyra exchanged a look. Ellie the hermit *owned* Gabrielle's?

"You seemed awfully upset when you saw my friend Ariana here unfrozen," Kyra said

"You broke into my store!" He started edging backward. "I should go to the constable right this minute."

"I don't think you want to do that." Kyra didn't have time to mess with a potion. Dropping the needle, she got into position to stop him with her body. "I think we should have a chat."

As Fred stood up, the hermit fumbled in his pocket and pulled out a fistful of potion tubes. "Don't step one foot closer! I've got weapons here that will put you all out for good! Stole them from her"—he gestured to Kyra with his chin—"so you know they're dangerous."

Kyra paused. He'd had the Peccant Pentothal in his room. Who knew what else he might have taken?

Ellie tossed two vials in the air and spun toward the door. Kyra lunged to catch them as Fred dashed after the old man. Unfortunately, Kyra dove directly in front of Fred, and they fell into a heap on the floor.

Kyra held a vial clutched tight in each hand.

Fred untangled himself and ran outside. He came back

moments later. "He's gone. Old man runs fast."

Kyra opened her hands.

"Oh-one two-three-three. Gas Relief. Must be one of Ned's. Can't eat that much pie without consequences." She turned the second bottle so she could read the label. "And 01 672. Sparkling Clean Dish Solution."

She felt so stupid. She couldn't get anything right. Now Ellie was out there somewhere, and they weren't any closer to having answers.

"Wow," Ariana said, "this really sucks."

"No kidding." Kyra brushed her long hair back with her hands. "Why in the world would he have kidnapped you? What could he possibly have to gain by it? He's just a crazy old guy who lives by himself."

Ariana shook her head and put the small portrait of Fred back into the locker. "So," she said, coming back to them. "What do we do now?"

"First, we get some sleep." Kyra said, her heart lifting a little at hearing Ariana's *we*. "Then we make a plan."

Fred, Ariana, and Kyra wound through the night-quiet streets of Wexford. Fred and Ariana spoke in hushed voices behind Kyra, Ariana's laugh occasionally bubbling up into the dark. By the time they entered the forest on the far side of the palace, their voices had grown louder and they seemed to be enjoying themselves.

"Keep it down!" Kyra hissed. She forced herself to think about something else.

 204

They needed to track down the fake princess, but it would help if first they knew what they were up against. What was she?

Kyra tried to open herself to her Sight, tried to focus it on the fake princess. But the only thing that flashed into her mind was the shriveled old face of the witch who had tried to kidnap them in the forest. She shivered; the witch had frozen her and Fred, just as Ariana had been frozen.

Was that why her image kept flashing into Kyra's head?

She thought about the false princess in her vision—looking down from her parapet while the world beneath her withered and turned black. Kyra took a sharp intake of breath. What was it the witch had said she'd been touched by? *An obeeka.*

"What's an obeeka?" Kyra asked.

Ariana said, "Oh, you know—kid's monster story. Parasite that sucks the life out of people." She waggled her fingers. "Oooh, scary!"

Fred laughed with her.

Kyra scowled and kept her thoughts to herself. What if obeekas *weren't* just storybook monsters? If an obeeka could suck the life out of those around it, why not suck the life out of an entire kingdom using the Nuptial Bond?

"I think I know what the imposter princess is," Kyra said. "Fred and I ran into a witch who told us an obeeka had touched me."

Ariana squinted. "Stupid obeeka should know better than to touch our Kitty."

"I'd hate to take the word of an evil witch who tried to eat us." Fred threw a stick for Langley. "Is this one of those Seer things?"

Kyra ignored his question as the woods gave way to a small clearing. "We're here," she said.

"Good thinking, Kitty," Ariana said. "I never would have thought of this."

"Is it just me or are we looking at a completely empty meadow?" Fred asked.

"It's just you," Kyra said. She began the process of dissolving the concealments hiding the tiny secret hut where she used to hide things for her adventures with Ariana.

She put her potions back in their bag and opened the door. "Beautiful, isn't it?"

Fred stepped inside the small shack and examined the dusty weapons hanging on the walls. "I'm glad we're on the same side."

"Me too," Ariana said.

Kyra walked around Fred to a trunk and pulled out some moth-eaten bedding. There was space for maybe two of them to sleep on the floor, but not much more.

"I'll sleep out here with Langley," Fred said. "You girls can have the luxury of sleeping under a roof."

"No, the royals should have the luxury of a roof," Kyra said, thinking it'd be easier to sneak away in the morning.

Kyra felt a hand on her back. "Don't even think about it." Ariana's voice came from behind her.

"I don't know what you're talking about."

"I know you—you're looking for a way to ditch us and go after this obeeka on your own."

Kyra turned to her friend. "If you got hurt, Ariana, I'd never forgive myself."

Ariana straightened, changing from a bedraggled-looking girl into the heir to the throne. "I want to save the kingdom too, Kyra. Promise me you'll give me a chance to do it."

Kyra finally nodded. "You've got my word."

It took Kyra some time to fall asleep even with the warm pig tucked in beside her.

The memory of Fred's—Ariana's *fiancé's*—kiss at the inn seared her. How could he do that knowing he was engaged to someone else?

The next morning, Kyra woke to the sound of birdsong, the crackle of a fire, and a lilt of two voices intertwining—

Fred and Ariana.

She stretched and felt for Rosie but found her bedroll empty. Light streamed in through the cracks around the door.

Outside, Fred was smiling his sunny smile at Ariana; Rosie was draped across her lap. The smoky smell of the fire was tinged with the sweet scent of something cooking.

Mmm, food.

"Kitty!" The princess interrupted her own stream of talk to pat the ground beside her. "You're still here."

Fred looked quizzically at Kyra. "Where else would she be?"

"You never know where you'll find our slippery kitty cat. Fred's making us breakfast."

Fred drizzled honey over a pan of springberries bubbling on the fire.

Kyra shivered in the cool morning, settling next to Ariana. She was still wearing the white blouse, and it didn't keep her as warm as her usual black shirt. But the soft fabric felt nice against her skin, so she'd resisted changing back.

Rosie opened an eye, and Kyra rubbed her cheek. The little pig shut her eye, lifting her cheek a fraction to give Kyra a better angle. Langley was chasing butterflies around the meadow.

Fred handed Kyra and Ariana warm biscuits. "So where do we start?"

Kyra took a bite and moaned happily. The springberries went perfectly with the toasty biscuits. Fred was a truly amazing cook. "I wish we knew more about what an obeeka can and can't do—if we're going to expose the fake princess, we need to be prepared." She wiped biscuit crumbs off her pants. "The only thing I really know about them is the old children's game called Face-stealer."

"We played that game!" Fred said, rocking back on his heels. "The Face-stealer is picked by drawing straws, secretly, then runs around tagging people. The idea is that no one knows who it is, see? You can't trust *anyone*. If the Face-stealer touches you, you fall to the ground. Last person standing wins." Fred nibbled a biscuit. "Stupid game. Our diplomats must have picked it up from Mohr."

"Or *our* diplomats picked it up from you." Ariana lobbed her biscuit at him.

"You know the game, princess?" Fred asked.

Ariana chuckled, bitterness showing on her face. "I wasn't allowed to play with other children."

"It's never too late." Fred smiled wickedly. "Up! I'll show you how it's done."

"It sounds like it's just running around."

"There are *skills* involved—skills of deception and treachery!"

Ariana set Rosie on the ground and took off running, Fred chasing her with a growl and the lumbering gate of a bear. Kyra had only ever played a few times. She hadn't been all that interested in courtyard games. But at least she'd had the chance. Ariana hadn't.

Ariana needed Fred. Not just to marry her and run the kingdom with her—she needed the fun, the playfulness that was all Fred.

They came back and flumped down, breathless. "Don't get too confident," Ariana said. "It was just my first game—next time I'll be prepared."

Kyra patted Ariana on the knee. "I'm sure you will, Ari."

"That game was not," Ariana said, "very instructive."

Fred took the pan off the fire. "But it *was* fun."

"I wish we knew who was involved," Kyra mused. "Someone helped the obeeka, and not just Ellie—someone inside the palace gave her the information she needed to imitate you. It could be anyone. We don't know who we can trust."

"Just like the game!" Ariana said, plucking a berry out of the pan. Juice dripped from her fingers.

"Who would benefit?" Fred asked. "Who's next in line for the throne after Ariana?" He handed her a clean red handkerchief from his pack.

"In Mohr, succession is through the female line. It would go to Mom's sister," Ariana said, making a face. "The Duchess Genria. Or to her daughter."

Kyra cracked a smile. "Believe me, the duchess's daughter is the least likely person in the world to be behind this."

"Why do you think that?" Fred asked.

"I've known her all my life," Ariana said. "Not a suspect."

"It could be anyone," Kyra repeated. She reached for the handkerchief to wipe her hands. "I think we need to find the fake princess before we'll know what to do next. I've been searching for her for months, though, and I have no idea where they're hiding her."

"I know where she is," Fred said.

"What?" Ariana and Kyra said at the same time.

"I'm full of untapped knowledge and wisdom." Fred folded his hands behind his head. "I am the groom, after all." He told them the story of how, while on his way to Mohr to start the whole pre-wedding business, a group of couriers had intercepted his traveling party. They'd had an urgent message about the assassination attempt, and redirected him to meet the princess at the ducal palace at Avon-on-the-River, where she was in protective custody. "Top secret and all that. Well, I wasn't going to be hemmed in like a poor nobleman who can't do a thing for himself. So I ditched my group and set off. I told everyone I was going to find the assassin myself, but I got a bit distracted." He lay back and crossed his legs. "Hey, the fishing in your kingdom is the best I've ever seen. You can't blame a guy."

"You're the man my parents have selected to be the next leader of the King's Army?" Ariana snorted.

"Apparently. I hope the soldiers like fishing."

"Does anyone know where you are?" Kyra asked Fred.

"Besides you two?"

"*That's* why they postponed the wedding." Kyra twisted the handkerchief into a knot. "It wasn't because of me trying to kill the princess at all. They lost the groom."

"The ducal palace," Ariana murmured. "Interesting place to hide the fake me."

"Why is that?" Fred asked.

"It's where the duchess lives with the duke when she isn't at the palace in Wexford."

"Which doesn't mean anything," Kyra said. "Except that Ariana and I have both been there, and we know a few ways to get in that aren't exactly common knowledge."

While Fred cleaned up, Ariana and Kyra went through the stock of weapons in the hut.

The walls were lined with a myriad of dangerous items—razor-thin rapiers, broadswords as tall and thick as Kyra's legs, maces, knives, throwing stars, and staves. There were so many spiky, deadly-looking things that the walls fairly glinted with menace.

They stood staring at the weapons, the faint sounds of Fred talking to Langley and the scraping of dishes floating in.

Ariana grabbed a little dagger from the wall. "So?" she demanded, startling Kyra.

"Soooo . . . what?" Kyra didn't look at her.

"What's the story with you and Hal?" Ariana flipped the dagger up in the air and caught it in her hand. "Still planning to marry the doofus when this is all said and done?"

Kyra plucked a sleek metal sword from a bracket on the wall. "It's over between me and the pretty idiot. The final straw was that he didn't trust my instincts about you, and now he's helping hunt me down. But it was over before that."

"Is fake me so convincing?" Ariana laid the dagger across her hand, checking the balance, then tossed it up, caught it, and threw it into a pocked practice board nailed to the wall.

"Not at all." Kyra experimentally swung a thin sword down one-handed and darted forward in the small space, testing the weight. "God, you should see the wedding dress fake Ariana had made. It is so incredibly hideous, it might actually make you throw up. But there was more to it than just the dress.

"I'd only been back a few days when I had the vision." Kyra's voice went quiet. "It was of you—or fake you—using the Nuptial Bond to suck the life right out of the kingdom. It was horrible, a vision of the world turned to black ash. I tried explaining to Hal, and he wouldn't listen. No one would believe me that something was wrong, not even your mother."

It was quiet in the hut. Ariana had stopped playing with the dagger. "Why didn't you ever tell me you were a Seer?"

"I couldn't. I knew how you felt about witches."

Here it was. All out on the table. Kyra wished she could dig a hole and hide in it rather than face her friend's condemnation.

Ariana had a puzzled look on her face. "What do you mean? We never talked about witches."

"That first day we met. You said they weren't even human."

"Kyra." Ariana reached over and put a hand on Kyra's arm. "I was *twelve*. I'd never even left my room. What did I know about anything?"

"I thought you'd stop being my friend if you found out."

Ariana pulled her into a hug. "Kyra, I don't know anything about witches, but if you're one, it must be a good thing."

Kyra's eyes welled up.

There was a cough behind them, then Fred's voice. "Are you two going to be hugging *every* time I walk into a room? I mean, I could get used to it, I just need to know."

Kyra pulled herself from Ariana's arms. "Don't you have something you need to be doing?"

"I just came for this." He grabbed a long staff off the wall. "I thought I should do some practicing before we storm any castles." He walked off with the staff over his shoulder, and the girls watched from the doorway as he began going through a series of drills.

Kyra's vision came back to her. There was the real Fred carrying one of her staffs, the tip glowing green with her poison. So her Sight hadn't lied to her about that.

She could only hope that her vision of the false Ariana and the dying Kingdom of Mohr never came true.

Twenty-three

WEAPONS STRAPPED TO THEIR sides and backs, tucked into sleeves and boot tops and leg holsters and anywhere else they could find, they set out toward the ducal palace. Kyra was back in her usual black clothing, her hair tied up tight, securely held in place with a wooden hair stick.

She followed behind Fred and Ariana, trying not to pay attention to the easy way the pair chatted and joked together. He was good for Ari, she reminded herself.

"Kyra?" Ariana said, over her shoulder. "Will you tell this pinhead how I'm the most knowledgeable person in the entire kingdom—and possibly the world—on the subject of hunting dogs, and if I say terriers are more reliable than hounds, I know exactly what I'm talking about?"

"She's the most knowledgeable person I know—at least on the subject of hunting dogs."

"See, I told you." Ariana smiled smugly.

"In fact, I wouldn't get her started, because she will go on and on for days."

"Kitty!"

"What she might NOT have mentioned is that she doesn't actually hunt with them. She has them flush out birds so she can watch them fly."

Ariana shot Kyra a dirty look before turning back to Fred. "Only the head groom knows, because I'm required to bring him with me. If you tell anyone, I swear you won't live to hear the laughing."

"Doesn't anyone notice that you don't come home with anything when you go hunting?"

"They just think I'm a terrible shot."

Fred laughed. Kyra couldn't see his face, but she knew that laugh, knew the smile that came along with it.

The small wooded path they were on broke out onto the edge of a large orchard abloom with apple blossoms before dipping back into the woods on the other side. Normally, Kyra would worry about being so out in the open, but she knew this area, and knew that the farmer would be working on his spring asparagus and pea crops on the other side of his land. Also, he was half deaf. She had been one of his customers when she'd lived in Wexford, making the hike out to buy his fruits and vegetables directly from him, and they'd mostly communicated by shouting at one another.

She pictured him standing in the sunshine in his work

clothes, a hat pulled low on his head—the perfect silhouette of a hardworking farmer.

Kyra was struck with an idea.

"Hey, Fred," she said, coming alongside the two royals. A gust of wind blew stray apple blossom petals around them. "How many changes of clothes do you have?"

"That's an awfully personal question."

"And yet, I still need to know the answer. If you aren't going to give it to me, I'll have to take your bag by force and rifle through it myself."

He held up his hands, fending her off. "I have some extra clothes."

"You're quick to give in," Ariana said. "You aren't afraid of our Kitty, are you?"

Kyra ignored her. "Perfect. We'll need two sets."

"I get it," Ariana said, picking up on Kyra's thinking as quickly as she always did. "You think we should dress as men, right?"

Kyra nodded. "I don't have any male glamours, so we're going to have to try disguises."

"Why don't you have any male glamours?" Fred asked.

"Because I never thought I could pull off being a man. It's not just about how you look, it's all about how you hold yourself and walk."

"How are you going to work a disguise if you can't do a glamour?"

"*You* are going to give us man lessons."

Ariana let out a sharp bark of laughter, her eyes twinkling. "Him? Are you kidding? *He's* going to give us man lessons?"

"We don't need to look super convincing as men close up," Kyra said. "We just need to give the impression of men Fred's taken into his service. If you saw a potion bottle with a red stamp on it, your brain would make you think it was a red skull, and you'd think it was dangerous even if the stamp was actually a grinning squirrel." Kyra looked at Fred skeptically. "I'm sure Fred can give us a *few* tips, at least, of how to act like men."

"Hey! I am more than capable of giving man lessons." Fred smiled broadly at Kyra. "What do you want to know?"

"For one thing, we need to know how to walk."

"No problem. I've been walking most of my life." Fred held up a hand. "Stop and watch."

The girls leaned up against an apple tree with Rosie at their feet.

"First, you aren't just acting like any kind of men; you're going to be especially manly men. I picked you up to work for me, after all, and I wouldn't choose just any men for that sort of thing. I need men who can fight and lift heavy things. You might want to spit occasionally."

"Why?"

"It helps keep you from looking too smart. Now, because you are so manly, it naturally follows that you have large upper-arm muscles. Huge muscles, really. The way you let people know this is by slightly bending your elbows and holding your arms out from your body, like your muscles are so big they're getting in the way."

Kyra and Ariana bent their elbows and pushed their arms a couple of inches away from their bodies.

The edges of Fred's lips quirked as though he was trying to restrain a smile. "Then you need to let them know that not only are you muscular, you're confident of your abilities in all areas. You accomplish this by swaggering when you walk. Langley, stay." He pointed for the dog to sit next to the girls.

Fred sauntered away from them under the lacey white boughs of the trees in a masculine strut.

"Your turn."

The girls copied Fred's walk while he stood back and watched.

"A little less hip swinging, Kyra."

"I'm not—"

"And don't walk so close together. Imagine there's at least one invisible guy between you at all times."

Ariana leaned over and whispered in Kyra's ear. "He wants us to imagine him between us. Guys are so weird."

"Men don't whisper, but if you have to do it, at least do it the right way."

Ariana and Kyra stopped walking and turned back to Fred.

"If you find you need to whisper, you don't get up close to the other person and lean into their ear. Stay where you are, a person's-width apart, and put a hand up on the far side of your face like a shield." He demonstrated with his hand out straight from one side of his face. "Then turn your head slightly to the other person and say what you need to say."

The girls exchanged a look.

"No 'best friends' glances at each other like that, either. Or 'dears' and 'darlings.' Men insult each other every chance they get."

"Men don't have best friends?" Kyra asked.

"You'd only know it by the ferocity of the insults. If a guy's your really good pal, you let him have it at every opportunity."

"Got it, fathead," Ariana said.

"Perfect." Fred plucked two blossoms from the tree above him and tucked one behind each girl's ear, then grabbed another and tucked it behind his own ear. "You have officially completed man lessons. Now that you know how to act like manly men, what's the plan?"

"You are the prince, at last come to claim your bride. You hired us to help you . . . fish, or whatever," Kyra said.

"But, Kitty, no one is going to be fooled by our manly acts," Ariana said.

"That's why we have to sneak past the guards. Royalty *never* looks closely at servants. But servants *do*, so we can't chance the guards blowing our cover. So, Fred, you're going to have to try to act princely."

"You know I really *am* a prince, Kyra." His green eyes sparkled as they met hers. "I didn't make that up."

"Fred, you're wearing a flower in your hair. It's kind of difficult to take you seriously," Ariana said. "We want people to immediately accept that you're Prince Frederick, here to marry the princess. If you act more royal, people won't think twice about us."

"Did you ever meet Prince Pompadou from Lexeter?" Ariana posed with one hand on her hip and pursed her lips, looking at them down her nose.

"Prince Pompous?" Fred asked.

"That's what we called him too!" Ariana said.

"I think I can add a little Prince Pompous to my act when we get to court." Fred rubbed his chin.

"We'll need hats," Kyra added. "I'm thinking Ari and I could wear them sort of low over our eyes to hide our hair and so people won't be able to make out our faces too well."

"I only have one hat," Fred said.

"No problem." Ari grinned and pulled a black-handled dagger out of her belt. "I've always wanted to do this." She grabbed a hunk of hair and sawed at it. A moment later she looked down at a golden swatch of hair in her palm. "This is great. Do you think I could make a mustache out of this?"

They reached the Pearl River at sunset. Kyra took in deep breaths of the clean smell off the water as they approached the bank. The waterway was wide here, about twenty sword-lengths across. "We're about a mile upstream from Avon-on-the-River and the ducal palace," she said. "This would be a good place to stop."

They'd chosen dinnertime to break into the palace, because the night watch wouldn't have been posted yet, and the daytime guards would be tired and sleepy. And they'd be able to count on the full court retinue being there to witness that there were two princesses when they revealed Ariana's identity.

"It's also not far to the miller's house," Kyra said. "Remember his wife, Ariana?"

"Super sweet, looks like a dumpling?"

"She's got a good heart and she can keep a secret. I think we should leave Rosie with her." Kyra couldn't look at either

of them. "There's no reason for Rosie to be a part of this. She's done her job. We can come back for her later."

They elected Ariana to go, reasoning that most people would have a difficult time saying no to their princess.

"We should give her a little something for doing us this favor," Ariana said. Both girls looked at Fred.

"Neither of you have money?"

"I've been on the floor of a dressmaker's shop, naked, for the past few months."

"And I've been on the run. My last stay in Wexford wiped me out."

Fred got out his purse and dropped a handful of coins into Ariana's palm.

"See if she has any pie she'd be willing to sell," Kyra instructed.

"Great idea." Ariana stretched her hand back out to Fred. "You're kidding."

"You try going months without food."

Fred put some more coins into Ariana's hand.

"It's really good pie," Kyra said.

Fred sighed and gave Ariana still yet more coins.

They set off for the miller's house. Kyra gave Rosie one last scratch and then stepped back to wait in the trees with Fred.

Langley moved as though to follow, but Fred held the dog back. "Sorry, pal, I wish you could stay there too, but I need to keep you with me. You complete my Prince Frederick look. Plus, you're good in a fight." He rubbed the dog's ears.

Kyra's throat clogged up as Ariana and Rosie walked up to the house beside the mill. She tried to swallow.

"It's okay to be attached to Rosie and want to take care of her," Fred said. "You don't have to hide that from me."

"I'm not hiding anything."

Up the hill, the miller's wife curtsied to Ariana.

"I think the miller's wife might be blushing," Kyra said, briskly changing the subject. "I guess it's not every day that the princess honors you with a visit."

"Ariana's pretty great."

Wrong subject. "Yeah, she is." Kyra's voice came out scratchy.

She kept her eyes on the house, where the miller's wife welcomed Ariana inside.

"Are you jealous?" Fred asked, shocking Kyra out of her misery.

"What? Why would I be jealous? That's absurd. Who do you think I'm jealous of?"

"Um—"

"I'm not jealous of anyone. Completely absurd."

"You already said that."

"Well, clearly I meant it."

Kyra bit her tongue to keep from saying anything more. She felt her face heating up.

"Okay," Fred said.

Okay? That was all he had to say? Kyra really wanted to punch him. Her thoughts raged: Was he talking about leaving the pig behind? Or was he talking about Ariana? Does he

care at all about me? If he cared, he wouldn't have given up so easily with his stupid "Okay."

She didn't want him to care anyway.

He belonged with Ariana.

She reminded herself of that back at the clearing by the river, when the two royals sat down next to each other and started preparing food together. Fred pulled bread and cheese out of his pack.

Ariana divvied up the pie.

Langley sniffed the shore, then started lapping water from the river's edge. He looked lonely without the pig beside him.

Kyra watched the Pearl River swirl by, the rush of water calming her nerves. She was getting better at ignoring the random images that came with her Sight, but they were still just barely tolerable. Could training actually help her control the visions? She shook the thought from her head. She was a *potioner*; she didn't have time for woo-woo witchy lessons just to make her day a little easier.

They ate and watched the river until the last bits of bread and cheese were gone.

Fred sprawled out on the ground beside Kyra, leaning back on his elbows. Ariana leaned back as well, and propped her feet on top of Fred's.

Kyra turned away and dug out a handful of feathers and some extra arrows she'd stowed in her pack.

The sun slowly sank down in the sky.

Fred got up and grabbed his pack. "I'm going to go get changed—I think, Kyra, even you will approve of my clothes.

They're much more 'princely' than these." He headed toward the bushes, turning back to say, "I know it will be difficult, but try to refrain from peeking."

He disappeared behind the screen of plants.

Ariana dabbed sap above her lip and smoothed a chunk of hair on each side, creating her mustache. "How does this look?"

"Um . . ."

"The only real answer to that is 'great.'"

"Looks great, Ari."

"Convincing and genuine?"

"Uh-huh?"

Fred popped out of the woods wearing a black riding outfit with a long navy velvet cloak attached at the shoulders. "Ariana, there's a small rodent on your face. Thought you should know."

"It's a mustache. Kyra has assured me that it's extremely convincing."

Fred shook his head and handed Kyra a suit of clothes. "You should take these—there's a belt you can use to cinch the pants, and I think the jacket will make you look a little bigger."

Kyra took the bundle. Fred pulled a hat out of his pack and plopped it on her head.

"Ew, it smells like fish."

Fred patted Kyra's head. "It's my lucky fishing hat. Never been washed."

Kyra sighed. "Let's go get changed, Ari."

Once full dark fell, they set out on the last leg of their

journey. The river shushed along beside them as they walked toward the palace.

Currents of energy coursed through Kyra—excitement mingled with fear. She tried not to think of all of the things that could go wrong.

At last they could make out the castle in the distance. Torches and potion-filled bulbs lit up its battlements, and the shadowy figures of guards stood on the ramparts and along the front gate.

Kyra, Ariana, and Fred made their way around to the back, staying in the shadows of the forest. The moon had grown round over the past few weeks, and cast down a bright white light.

"There's a tunnel hidden there," Kyra explained in a whisper, pointing to a shrine built on the backside of the outer castle wall. "Just behind that bush and the statue of the Goddess of Compassion. It's for the duke and his family to flee during a siege, or to sneak in supplies."

There was a stretch of open ground between them and the wall.

"The guards do their rounds on the hour and the half hour. The ones up on the ramparts on the quarter to and quarter of. Our best bet will be to make a run for it after one set of guards has passed and before the next one shows. There," Kyra said as the duke's chapel bells began ringing. "It sounds like we're right on the hour. The ground crew should be by any minute."

They waited. The statue of the Goddess of Compassion shone silvery white in the moonlight, one hand in her lap

and the other held up in a posture of forgiveness. There were flowers at her feet and some lying gently in the stone folds of her robe.

The guards didn't come. Kyra could almost feel Fred and Ariana holding their breath on either side of her. Langley leaned against Kyra's legs, and she reached down to rub the top of his head, half wishing Rosie were with them.

No, she reminded herself. It was better that Rosie was somewhere safe.

"Should we make a run for it before the quarter hour hits?" Ariana asked quietly.

Kyra hesitated, a feeling of unease growing inside her. There was a chance that they'd changed security since she'd last been here. If she was wrong about this, what else could she be wrong about?

"Okay," she said to Ariana. "Let's go."

They darted out into the open.

"Halt!" A voice shouted from the side.

The guards had just been running late. Kyra cursed inwardly and pulled out two Doze-tipped throwing needles as she turned toward the sound of the voice.

Two men were running toward them, spears in hand.

Thwip. Thwip.

Kyra's needles whipped through the air, and both figures fell to the ground. "We've got to be fast," she said, "and we have to hide them before the guards above see."

Fred and Ariana ran to the fallen men, Fred slinging one over his shoulder and Ari picking up the arms of the other, leaving the legs for Kyra.

 227

The two girls heaved the limp body up and followed Fred and Langley toward the hidden entrance to the tunnel.

"Now, that," Kyra said, pointing her chin to the guy they were carrying, "is a real mustache."

"What are you talking about?" Ariana looked down at the bushy facial hair of the guard. "It looks just like mine."

They had just reached the Goddess of Compassion when the quarter-hour bell began to ring.

"Fred, come help me with this." Kyra dropped the guard's legs and went to the shrine. Extending out from either side of the goddess statue was what looked like a large moss-covered stone base. She moved her hands under the flat rectangle. "Right here." Fred placed his hands next to hers. "On the count of three, heave up."

Fred's shoulder brushed against Kyra's as he positioned himself to lift the stone.

And a waft of that spicy-forest Fred smell hit her.

She shook her head—she didn't have time to moon over her best friend's fiancé. Why, she wondered, did he have to smell so tasty?

"One, two, three." She and Fred lifted the stone up and to the side, revealing a staircase that led into darkness.

"Wow." Fred looked down into the black hole. "I never would have known this was here. The moss is a nice touch."

Kyra couldn't help smiling at him as he slung the guard he'd been carrying back over his shoulder and disappeared down the hole.

When his head popped back into view, the girls passed down the second guard. Langley sniffed the edge of the

opening and attempted a tentative step on the stairs. He pulled back and gave Kyra a heartbreaking look.

"He'll be back, pal. Fred's not going to leave you here alone."

Fred reappeared, and Langley's tail started wagging.

Fred hugged his wolf dog to his chest, then turned and carried him down.

"Ari, you head in," Kyra told her. "I can get the top back on by myself."

Ariana squeezed Kyra's shoulder as she went past and scrambled down the stairs.

Kyra followed, steadying herself on the narrow steps before reaching up. The slab had been counterweighted in such a way that it was easier to reposition the stone from below than to lift it from above. Kyra's muscles strained, but at last it thudded into place.

And cut off the sound of the next set of chapel bells ringing.

Twenty-four

AT THE FOOT OF THE NARROW STAIRS, Fred and Ariana were each lighting a lantern they'd taken from hooks along the tunnel walls.

"There should be two sets of guards in this part of the castle," Kyra whispered, her voice echoing softly in the confined space. "One set roams this wing of the palace, and the other is stationed just down the way at the doors to the main hall. If we time it right, we should be able to take out both sets of guards at the same time."

They crept along the cool dark passage, Langley's claws clicking against the cobbled floor. Fred's and Ariana's lanterns cast quivering shadows as they walked.

At the end of the tunnel they came to a dead end. To the

right was a large hook to hang a lantern on, looping up to a curling iron head, but Kyra knew better. She pointed to the iron ring, whispered, "Lever," and the princess put a hand on the loop in immediate understanding.

Kyra positioned herself, a needle in each hand, and listened for movement.

When the sound of footsteps grew close, Kyra nodded to Ariana. The princess pulled the ring, and the wall at the end of the hall swung open—it was a hidden door made of the same stone as the palace walls.

On the other side were two startled guards. Kyra stepped out and stabbed her needles into their arms, and they slumped to the ground.

"Hey!" shouted one of the two men posted outside the doors to the main hall. Kyra pulled her arm back and threw hard, her needle flying true and striking him in the shoulder. She followed that one with another needle.

Both men fell.

Kyra and her friends waited, listening for responses to the shout. When none came, they quickly moved to hide the bodies of the sleeping guards in the tunnel and pulled shut the secret door. It blended seamlessly.

They crouched down outside the closed doors of the main hall.

Kyra could hear the buzz of talk and laughter from inside. The duke liked people to enjoy themselves at the ducal palace—no one went hungry or lacked for entertainment behind these walls.

Ariana peeked through the crack between the heavy,

carved wooden doors, a look of fascinated horror on her face. "She's here, at the duke's table at the far end. She's wearing a poufy, baby blue dress and looks absolutely horrid. Ugh, do I really look like that?"

Fred squinted, his head to the side of Ariana's. "How you look isn't about the face you were born with, it's what you do with it. Don't worry, you don't look anything like her."

"Oh, my—Kitty, see who's sitting next to the duke?"

Kyra pushed between the two royals and peered through the crack. "The Duchess Genria. Of all the times for her to choose to be by her husband's side. Fred, you better hope she doesn't recognize you as the slow fellow she met outside that barn."

"Not with my Prince Frederick act."

"Ready?" Kyra asked. They arranged themselves, Kyra to the left and Ari to the right of Fred, with Langley taking the lead.

Fred winked at Kyra.

Kyra and Ari pushed open the doors, allowing Fred to enter the hall.

The smoky air smelled of roasted meat and candle wax. There was a roaring open fire to one side, a dozen dining tables with chandeliers over them, and long tapestries hanging above the duke's long table at the end of the hall.

Conversations in the room carried on as the three of them proceeded down the center aisle, but Kyra felt curious eyes on her as people checked out the group. She had to keep herself from reaching up to make sure her hat was as far down on her forehead as it could go.

When they were a half-dozen feet away from the duke, they were halted by two uniformed men. The duke was a robust-looking man with rosy cheeks and a round belly that filled out his evening garments. There was a giant platter of roasted meat in front of him, with fat candles guttering on either side. The crowd in the hall hushed.

The guards barred their way with long spears. To their left a soldier with curly black hair said, "Why weren't you accompanied by the door crew?"

"I have my own accompaniment, thank you," Fred said regally.

"Please state your name and business," the guard said.

Kyra swept her arm in Fred's direction and lowered her voice. "His Royal Highness, Prince Frederick Lantana the Third, of Arcadia."

Fred inclined his head toward the duke. The older gentleman looked pleased but didn't respond. As though he were waiting for something.

Kyra saw a flash of panic on Fred's face. He gestured downward with his hand.

They were so busy trying to look like men, Kyra and Ari had forgotten their courtly manners. Kyra put her hand up on the far side of her face as a shield, just as Fred had taught her, and, without moving any closer to Ari, she whispered, "He wants us to bow."

Ari put her hand up on the far side of her face and whispered back, "What?"

"Bow, you nitwit," Kyra whispered louder, remembering to add a manly insult.

 233

Several people in the hall tittered.

"Oh," Ari said.

They both bowed low at the waist. When they came back up, Kyra noted that the duke had taken the opportunity to sneak a swig from his oversized wine goblet. The duchess's eyes narrowed, and Kyra felt her stomach clench in response.

"Your Graces," Fred began, addressing the duke and duchess with his chest puffed out. "I can't tell you how pleased I am to make your acquaintance. And, Your Highness, to finally see your beauty in person is an honor. I apologize for the lateness of my arrival. I have traveled across the Kingdom of Mohr, hoping to do my part to ensure the princess's safety by tracking down her would-be assassin, but alas, I found nothing on my travels. I can only present my humble self to you and hope that it is enough."

Kyra watched the fake princess, but couldn't read the expression on her face.

"The prince!" the duke said, chuckling. "Finally. You had us worried, young man."

The guards lowered their spears, and Fred took a few casual steps forward with his dog, Kyra, and Ariana right behind him.

"I am deeply grieved to hear it," Fred said. "And shamed to say that I've had the time of my life. I have made the most interesting of acquaintances. I'll allow them to introduce themselves."

The duchess's gaze on them didn't soften, but the duke looked intrigued at the idea of being introduced to the two commoners in front of him.

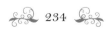 234

Ariana stepped forward and whipped off her mustache. "Ha-HA!" she said.

Kyra shook her head. Ari was having way too much fun with this.

"Uncle, it is I, your niece, the real Princess Ariana!"

Gasps sounded from the crowd.

This was the distraction Kyra had been waiting for. She pulled out her throwing needle, but the fake princess had already found her feet and taken off, running toward the side door of the hall.

A nobleman at the end of the table lunged for Kyra as she bounded forward in pursuit of the fake princess, but she threw a side kick to his chest that sent him flying, and kept going.

Kyra's hat flew off as she sped after the girl, and she heard more gasps as pieces of her long dark hair tumbled out of her bun and down her back.

She darted out the side door and into a narrow service hall, the light from the wall lanterns illuminating her path.

A glimpse of the princess's baby blue dress flitted into the dark off to the right.

Kyra followed, but there were no lanterns lit down this hall, so she fished out her necklace. Even with its glow, she could only see a foot or so ahead.

Tick, tick, tick. A lady's high-heeled shoes clicked somewhere in front of her.

A door slammed.

Kyra reached the end of the dark hall and felt the heavy studded metal bands on the door.

The dungeon.

Kyra opened the door and raced down the stairs in the dark, almost running into the false princess at the bottom of the steps. Kyra grabbed her wrist and jabbed a needle dipped in sleeping draft into her forearm.

The false princess didn't react at all, except to look down curiously at the needle sticking out of her arm. "Hmm," she said. "Not nice."

Kyra's next thought flew through her head like an arrow: I *didn't* miss. My needle had flown true when I threw it at the princess at her party.

These obeeka creatures were immune to Doze. Even at full-fatal strength.

The glowing necklace around Kyra's neck suddenly grew heavy, until it felt as though it weighed a thousand pounds.

The dark eyes of the false princess watched, smiling, as Kyra fell to her knees on the dungeon floor. "I guess you don't have the best magic after all, *Master Potioner*." She laughed and turned away. Her shoes tapped up the stairs, and the door slammed shut, echoing through the dungeon.

Kyra was alone in the darkness.

She tried to reach up to take the necklace off, but whatever made it so heavy also affected her body—her hands weighed too much to raise them to her chest. Soon Kyra was spread flat on her back, her arms and legs immobile against the damp stone beneath her. Even her skin felt leaden, the weight of her face dragging down her lips and stopping her from being able to scream.

Her mind moved slowly, as though the heaviness of her body somehow slowed down the processes of her brain too.

The necklace had been charmed to stop her if she grabbed the fake princess.

Why would Hal have planned to give her something like that? He'd said it was intended to be a gift. A gift for the relationship they'd had before. That didn't make any sense. But . . .

He'd bought it at a new stall at the Saturday market.

New stall.

For being one of the smartest and most talented potioners around, sometimes Hal was so stupid.

Kyra's move back to Wexford had alarmed whoever was behind this. And in order to stop the princess's best friend, a known poisonous weapons expert, from interfering with the false princess, they'd taken a chance that Hal might give a shiny necklace to his fiancée.

Something scurried across the floor near Kyra's head.

Her mind filled with images of rats and spiders and creepy-crawly things that lived in the dark. They could walk right across her without her being able to stop them. *Ugh.*

The door at the top of the stairs opened with a click. Footsteps pounded down.

A dog's tongue licked the side of Kyra's face.

Fred appeared above her. "Stay back, Langley." He pulled the big dog away. "There's something wrong with her. Kyra? Can you move?"

Fred. Lovely, lovely Fred.

"I'll take that as a no." He checked her eyes and ran his hands along her heavy arms. "It doesn't seem like anything's broken."

He must *figure this out.*

"There has to be something going on here that I can't see."

The necklace—come on, Fred, it isn't that hard, see the nice glowy thing on my chest?

"I need more light." Kyra could hear him rifling through his bag, then he appeared above her again, his hair rumpled like he'd been rubbing his hands over it. "I wonder if it's safe to move you."

His lips moved as he was thinking, just slightly. She'd never have noticed it if she wasn't completely immobile watching him.

He wasn't going to figure this out.

She was going to be here forever.

"If I could just see around you, check for some signs of what kind of spell is doing this."

His hands touched her necklace.

Yes!

"I'm just borrowing this so I can see if there's anything on you that's causing this. Don't be mad, okay?"

Gently, he lifted the necklace from Kyra's chest. Sliding one hand beneath her leaden head, he strained to pull her head up and slide the chain under.

Kyra gasped.

The enormous weight had been lifted. She sat up. "Thank the gods. I thought you'd never figure it out!"

"You are always so gracious when rescued."

"Please, get rid of that thing." Kyra glared at the necklace. "I don't ever want to see it again. How did you find me?"

"I left Ari to explain things to the duke, and followed you to keep back any pursuers. I almost lost track of you, it was so dark! But then I saw a tiny, almost unnoticeable glow, and there you were. What happened to the fake princess?"

"There was some kind of spell on the necklace to stop me from hurting her. Once I dropped, she took off."

The *tick, tick, tick* of a lady's shoes sounded again on the stairs, causing them both to jump.

"Did you leave the door open?" Kyra whispered.

"Yes?"

"Damn."

A long line of cells was behind them, but there was no back exit. Kyra slid a needle from her holster and braced herself. Fred quietly raised his staff.

The light from a lantern threw shadows on the wall.

The beautiful face of the Duchess Genria appeared.

Kyra slumped down. "Hi, Mom."

Twenty-five

WHY COULDN'T IT HAVE been anyone other than her mother? Fighting any one of the highly skilled guards at the castle would be preferable to dealing with the Duchess Genria.

The one nice thing Kyra could say about her mom was that she had forced her to become friends with her cousin Ariana—even if it *was* for a silly reason like sharing cosmetics charms.

Before that, Kyra hadn't been allowed to meet her cousin at all, even though her room in the palace was only three halls away. And two staircases, and a dumbwaiter.

But the queen hadn't wanted to take any chances with her daughter, so only her husband, her sister the duchess, medical professionals, and Ariana's nurse were allowed to see the princess.

The young Kyra would sit hidden under a staircase just down the hall from the princess's room and wait to catch a glimpse of her.

More often than not, she heard only screeching and tantrums.

But who could blame her cousin for throwing tantrums when she was all locked up like that? Kyra was sure that if they met they'd be best friends. They were cousins, the same age, and they both lived in the palace. It was *perfect*.

So Kyra was forever grateful to her mother for helping her and the princess become best friends. But *gratitude* wasn't the same as *trust*; she knew better than most that the Duchess Genria did nothing that didn't benefit herself in some way.

The duchess descended the stairs to the dungeon slowly, each of her steps regal.

Fred bumped his shoulder against Kyra's. "Did you just call the duchess 'Mom'?"

"Um, yeah."

The duchess stepped off the last step and addressed Kyra. "Why do you insist on trying to kill your cousin?"

"I'm not trying to kill my cousin!"

The duchess raised one fine eyebrow. "Just now you chased the princess through the hall. Don't tell me you weren't trying to kill her."

"Mother," Kyra said, "if you ever listened to me *at all*, you would know that something strange was going on with

Ariana. That person I was chasing *isn't* my cousin. Didn't you notice that there was another Ariana who was WITH me?"

"Can we back up a minute?" Fred asked. "The duchess is your *mother*? I thought you said you'd run away from home."

"You told him you ran away from home?" the duchess said.

"I did!"

The duchess chuckled. "Well, you didn't run very far, did you, dear? The Potions Academy is practically connected to the castle."

"You didn't talk to me for two years! Not until you thought I'd be useful to you by 'socializing' Ariana."

"*Pffft!* You've always been so imaginative. Can't understand where you got that from. Probably your father. Do you have any idea what you've done to him? Our physician is upstairs with him right now trying to calm him down."

Fred interrupted. "And the princess is your cousin? Am I getting this right?"

"Yes, Fred," Kyra said. "Ariana is my cousin."

"Doesn't that make you . . . ?"

"A princess," the duchess said. "I was born a princess, so my daughter is a princess, as well. Of course, I prefer to go by *duchess*, my married title. *Princess* sounds so young. *Fluffy*." She shuddered. "Kyra has always eschewed proper titles. She could at least go by Lady Kyra, but no, not our *Master Potioner*." The Duchess snorted. "She not only insisted on blemishing the family name by working, she had to go and claim the potioner title." The duchess clapped her hands together. "Enough. You're coming with me."

"You're going to turn me over to the king's soldiers?"

"We need to get things straightened out. Come along."

"No." Kyra took a step back, pulling Fred along beside her. "I'm not going anywhere with you. You'll have me hanged."

"Kyra," Fred said, exasperated, "she's your *mom*. She's not going to let them hang you."

"Look, Mother, I know that witch was working for you. You had her attack us—she was going to *eat* me. I'm not going anywhere with you."

"She tried to *eat* you?" The beautiful features of the duchess twisted in disgust. "You must be mistaken. She was probably just trying to scare you."

"She was going to eat us. Before that, she tried to enslave us."

"That woman needs to learn some restraint. I told her to keep anyone unusual traveling through the forest until I got there. I shouldn't have had to specify that they should remain *whole*. I pay that witch good money, but she's always looking out for herself."

So intent was Kyra on her mother's blasé rant about the witch that she didn't notice the soldier sneaking down the stairs behind her.

He appeared beside the duchess, one of Kyra's own needles in his hand.

As Kyra went to lift the one she held, she felt a small prick on her shoulder.

"That's not fair!" she protested, just as everything went black.

Twenty-six

Kyra woke up with a pounding headache.

They'd used her own sleeping draft against her. Those jerks.

She was cold too. And whatever she was lying on was hard.

She opened her eyes to find herself in one of the cells in the dungeon, lit by only a small torch that guttered on the wall outside the bars of her cell. She sat up and felt for her weapons—all gone. She'd been stripped of her needle holster, her knives, her powder pockets, everything.

This was so not how things were supposed to go.

What were Ariana and Fred doing? Were they in the dungeon too?

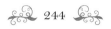

"Hello?" Kyra called, her voice echoing off the walls. "Hello?"

The only response was some intense squeaking and scurrying sounds. Her skin crawled.

What if they left her here to starve?

That would be worse than hanging.

By the time she heard the sound of someone coming down the dungeon steps, her body ached from her hunched-over position on the hard floor, she was freezing, and her head still hurt. She stood woozily, backing up into the far corner. Her head struck the wall, and something dug into her scalp.

They'd missed her hair stick.

Kyra drew it out, her long hair falling down her back, and pushed the button to pop out the blade. She moved up beside the cell door.

When the door swung open, Kyra leaped out and grabbed the person, yanking him around so that he stood in front of her, her blade to his throat. Her other hand clasped rich velvet.

The duchess.

"Kyra, this is ridiculous. Take your little blade away, dear. I've come to let you out."

"You're just going to march me right upstairs and let me go? I don't believe that. You tried to track me down for the king, you sent a witch after me, you're probably going to let me hang."

"Is that what you really think?"

Kyra didn't say anything. *Of course* it was what she really

thought—but her mom made it sound stupid.

"I was trying to track you down," the duchess said slowly, "because I was worried about you. I would never have let the king or his soldiers harm you. I'm your *mother*, Kyra, not a monster."

"Then why am I locked up in this dungeon?"

"I'm afraid the soldiers were a little overzealous. It has taken all of my diplomatic skills to sort this out. Your friends were absolutely no help. They have all the grace of a couple of angry bears. I don't know how they're to be expected to run a country someday."

"Is that what this is all about, Mother? Are you behind this? You don't think Ari should run the country?"

The duchess made a *tsk*ing sound. "I'm not behind anything. Ariana will do a fine job, but she is definitely still in need of some serious training when it comes to dealing with people. Do you really think I would hurt my own niece?"

"You're using your gift on me, aren't you?" Kyra demanded. "Trying to charm me."

"I'm your mother, I don't need to charm you. Kyra, please put the blade down and come upstairs. Your cousin Ariana is currently chained to a table beside her double. Your bag is up there—you have a vial of your truth serum in it, don't you? Ariana said you did, but as we're taking the matter very seriously, we aren't trusting either one of them."

Kyra thought back to the creatures of Arlo Abbudato's she'd met in the woods. "These things don't react to potions the same way that people do, Mother—I don't even know if my serum will work."

"Well, then, we'll just have to hope that it *does*." The duchess shook a vial in her hand. "I believe this is the antidote to the headache caused by your sleeping potion?"

Kyra popped her blade back into her holster and reached for the vial. "How'd you know?"

"I do pay attention sometimes. I found it in your room upstairs."

The duchess turned to face Kyra, touching her throat where the blade had rested. "Don't think I'm going to forget this little incident. You are in serious trouble, young lady, for turning a weapon on your own mother."

Kyra wound her hair back up, replaced the stick, and swallowed hard. She would rather face another witch or a whole pack of Arlo Abbaduto's men than see the punishment her mother had in store for her.

"Sorry," she said.

But her mother only *humph*ed and said, "Come along."

Kyra's mother brought her to her father's sitting room, which he used primarily for drinking spirits and gaming with his friends after dinner. The ducal palace didn't have a courtroom of any kind.

Today, instead of a stack of cards or a chessboard, the gaming table had shackles bolted to it. Side by side, their wrists cuffed to the table, were two Princess Arianas.

Kyra ignored the baby-blue-frocked Ariana and nodded to the Ariana dressed in Fred's clothes.

The room was filled with people—regular folk, soldiers, guards, and nobles. Fred and Langley stood beside the duke's

favorite stuffed chair, and the duke himself sat in it, a yellow handkerchief in one hand to mop his face, and a glass of amber-colored liquid in the other. The duke's eyes lit up at the sight of Kyra, but he suppressed the grin that threatened.

These were serious proceedings.

Dartagn greeted Kyra and passed over her potions bag. The guard seemed to pop up everywhere she was.

Kyra took a seat across from the two princesses. Taking out the vials, she began her dilution of 07 211, Peccant Pentothal—the vial of poison she'd found carelessly thrown under Ellie's couch, the poison used to transform her friend, the poison with which she'd almost killed Arlo Abbaduto.

This time, there would be no mistakes.

Kyra painstakingly checked the measurement of every drop in the dilution medium. She added her alkalines and gently stirred in her colloids and worked through the process in complete silence. She loathed using the serum on Ariana again and risking her life, but there was only one way to uncover the truth. Kyra would get it right this time.

She had to.

Carefully, she swirled the diluted poison around in the vial and picked up her dropper. She prayed that this poison—unlike Doze—would have some effect on the obeeka.

She squeezed one drop on each princess's shackled left hand.

The effects were immediate.

The Ariana in the poufy blue dress began transforming—her blond ringlets darkened and lost their curl, and she began to shrink. A loud gasp filled the room as the false princess dwindled into a small childlike creature with unblinking black eyes, its hands almost—but not quite—small enough to escape the shackles. An obeeka.

Identical to the creatures Kyra had encountered at Arlo Abbaduto's lair.

Of course he was behind it. He'd replaced the princess with one of the shape-shifters in his employ. He'd known about the properties of Red Skull Serum when mixed with pine oil. He'd engineered the whole thing.

"You work for Arlo Abbaduto?" Kyra demanded.

The obeeka grimaced and tried to pull out of the cuffs. "He's not going to stand for this!" Its voice sounded like a whole crowd of people talking in synchrony. It made Kyra's skin crawl.

She had gone to Arlo for *help.* Now Rosie's failure to find the princess the first time around made perfect sense—Arlo had never wanted to help her. He just wanted her to cover his tracks. So he'd put something in the basket that would lead her to another of his puppets, Ellie the hermit. Maybe he thought Kyra would kill the old man. Or that Ellie would kill Kyra.

"I think the king is going to have some questions for you," Kyra said to the creature.

"You won't be able to hold me. You don't even know what I am."

"Dartagn?" Kyra called.

"Yes, my lady?" He appeared at her side.

"Release Princess Ariana from her shackles immediately."

Dartagn made a gesture, and a soldier unlocked the iron bands.

"We're going to need to reinforce the prisoner's shackles," Kyra said. "It's an obeeka and can change shape to slip out of bonds. In my rooms, I have a potion that will force it to maintain this shape, and an anti-rot concoction we were trying out in the gardens last summer that could keep it from degenerating its shackles."

Dartagn sent a pair of soldiers to fetch the potions, and assigned two others to keep watch on either side of the creature.

Kyra stood up.

"You might have me," the creature said, "but you'll never find my master. Not if you interrogate me all day. I don't know where Arlo is."

"We'll see," Kyra said. She looked at the soldiers. "Just in case it might be dangerous, you should take it to the dungeon for the interrogation."

The two men unbolted the creature's shackles from the table and led it out.

The room erupted in applause and whistles, and people shouted her name.

Kyra felt a blush spread across her face.

The duke stood up and raised a hand for silence, his rosy cheeks glowing. "Thank you all for being here to witness this event. Our princess is safe, and a sinister plot has been uncovered that would have destroyed the kingdom we all know and love.

"I want to thank my daughter, Kyra, for persevering in the face of all obstacles. Darling, I'm so proud of you."

Kyra thought she caught her mother roll her eyes from

across the room, but figured she had to be imagining it. The sentiment might be there, but her mother would *never* do something so undignified.

The duke clapped his hands. "Drinks! We must have drinks to celebrate!"

Ariana linked an arm through Kyra's and whispered in her ear, "You know, kitty cat, you don't need to go to such great lengths to find out my secrets. I'd tell you anything you wanted to know without a truth serum."

"Ari, maybe we should get you out of here. No joke. You really are dangerous with this truth serum in you. You might say something you wished you hadn't."

"Like that your mom scares me, but I think your dad is kind of cute, in an old-guy sort of way?"

"Exactly like that."

"Eh." She shrugged. "I'm not worried."

The tension in the room lifted, and everyone erupted into conversation and laughter as drinks were produced and trays piled high with cheese and meat were brought around. A few people bowed to Kyra as they passed, or lifted their glasses to her when they caught her eye.

Kyra watched while, across the room, Fred taught her dad his fish song. The duke laughed uproariously as Fred got to the part about ducking his head under the water and tipped his ale over his face and spluttered. Her dad immediately reached for his mug to try it himself.

Beside her, Ariana laughed, then disentangled herself from Kyra to rush toward the men, shouting, "Save some for me!"

Ariana smiled up at Fred as he mimed along with the duke singing through the song, spilling ale extravagantly all over his face.

Kyra shut her eyes, but the image of her two friends enjoying each other's company didn't go away. She edged toward the door, a smile fixed on her face as each person she passed congratulated her.

She accepted the praise but kept moving.

"Princess," came a deep voice behind her.

Kyra turned to the drooping-mustached man behind her. "Dartagn."

"I'm glad you've made everything right, princess."

"You know I hate it when you call me that."

Dartagn's eyes glowed. "I know."

"Dartagn, did you really believe I'd kill my best friend for no reason?"

He shook his head. "Of course not. I trust you. Why else do you think you were one of our special combat trainers? I don't invite just anyone to do that." He paused. "Did you really believe I hadn't found you in the woods?"

Kyra's jaw dropped.

"I knew my trust in you was not misplaced."

"You knew where I was all this time?"

He nodded.

It shouldn't have made such a difference that her combat teacher trusted her, but it did. She smiled and turned and was at last out of the room.

In the empty hall, she leaned against the smooth stone wall.

 252

She was going to have to pull herself together. Everything was great now, right? Her best friend was alive and happy. She was no longer a fugitive. She'd saved the kingdom.

If everything was so great, why did she feel so terrible?

Her two friends were engaged to be married. And if Kyra had ever had any doubt that it would be a successful match, it was quickly evaporating.

Ariana was falling for Fred. And from the looks of it, Fred was falling for her too.

Twenty-seven

THEY WERE UP BEFORE DAWN the next day.

Kyra and her friends joined Dartagn and a contingent of the duke's guards on the road to the royal palace in Wexford. The party was quiet as they made their way to the castle, as though they'd used up their share of joy the night before. Kyra had knots in her stomach as she thought about what lay ahead.

Even picking up Rosie from the miller's wife didn't relieve the tension building in her.

The closer they got to the castle, the more she worried.

No matter the reason, she had tried to kill the princess. Would the king and queen understand? Would they believe her?

Ariana was back in her own clothes, and her hair had been prettily pinned by one of the duchess's maids. When they reached the front gate of the castle, the guards lowered their weapons at the sight of Dartagn and their princess.

Kyra looked up at the ramparts and groaned. "Maybe you should go ahead and explain."

"It's going to be fine," Ariana whispered, taking Kyra's hand. "You're the hero. They aren't going to throw you in the dungeon. I won't let them."

"Thanks, Ari." They made their way with Rosie down the curving walk to the palace entrance.

Fred came up behind them and put a hand on their shoulders. "You'll make sure they won't throw me in the dungeon too, right, Ari? I did sort of disappear there—not the best way to make a first impression on foreign royalty. . . ."

"We'll see," Ariana responded cheerfully.

She led them through the tall arched front doors of the castle and into the receiving room, while Dartagn went ahead to inform the king and queen.

Kyra sat on one of the sofas. Rosie curled up on a tasseled pillow.

No one spoke.

At last, the door swung open and in walked the king in full regal dress, his crown firmly planted on his head, the queen trailing behind.

"So," the king boomed, "I hear we have a plot on our hands."

Kyra stood up and bowed to the royal couple. "Your Majesty?" Her heart in her throat, she straightened.

The king's eyes were on her, and she couldn't look away. "I hope you're planning to see this thing through, young lady," he said. "Dartagn insisted you be the one to lead the party to capture Arlo Abbaduto. I can't help but agree. No one is braver, truer, or more capable."

Relief flooded through Kyra.

The queen stepped up beside the king. "But don't even think for a minute that this party will include *you*, young lady," she said to Ariana. "Or you," she said to Fred. "I can't imagine what your parents would say if they heard you'd been involved with this."

The king opened his arms to his daughter. "We're so relieved to have you back." Ariana accepted the hug while her mother patted her shortened locks.

"So short, Ariana! Was this really necessary?"

"Of course it was, Mom. You don't think I'd have done it if it hadn't been, do you?"

A wry smile appeared on the queen's face. She knew just how little reason the princess needed to shear off her hair.

The king gave his daughter one last squeeze, then pulled back. "We've got work to do."

Within a few hours, Kyra was standing in the sun-dappled woods north of the city, surrounded by a contingent of the King's Army, who were going to assist in the capture of Arlo Abbaduto. Two members of the team had been a surprise to Kyra. They weren't soldiers.

They were potioners.

Hal and Ned.

They'd come up to her beforehand, looking like puppies who'd eaten her slippers.

"Kyra," Hal said. "I'm so sorry. We—"

"It's okay," Kyra said. "I wish you'd trusted me, but I don't hold it against you."

"I would if I were you," Hal said. "I was a fool. You always *were* too headstrong for me."

"And you never were . . ."

He waited. "Yes? Never what?"

"I don't know. *Enough*, I guess? Sorry," Kyra said.

He nodded and said, "True."

"I'm glad you're back, Kyra." A grin took over Ned's wide face. "Hal's been driving me nuts."

Kyra smiled. "I'm glad to be back."

"We're in this together, right?" Hal said.

"Yeah, Hal, we're in this together." It was shocking to her to realize she meant what she said.

"Arlo is a formidable enemy," Kyra began, speaking to the team. "We cannot underestimate him. Hopefully, we'll have the element of surprise, because wherever he's hiding, we'll find him. We've got this."

She held up a small container—one she'd kept since her dealings with the King of Criminals. Something inside it rattled angrily, like a bug in a box. "Inside is a potioners' coin, one of a handful I paid to Arlo a few weeks ago. I changed the owner's imprint over to him, but I held on to one of the coins . . . as an insurance policy. I didn't know whether I could trust him or not."

One of the soldiers snorted.

"Of *course* I couldn't trust him," she added, and the group broke into quiet laughter. "This coin, once released, will do whatever it can to find Arlo."

Potioners' coins were driven by two distinct traits: a need to be with their owners, and sneakiness. They waited until there was no chance that anyone would notice, then they slipped out of the till or pocket they'd been put in and slowly found their way back home. But the coins weren't *smart*— they were easy to fool. Kyra knew that all she had to do was pretend to look the other way.

She opened the container, fished the coin out, and set it on the ground. Then she made a great show of crossing her arms and looking up at the treetops.

Out of the corner of her eye she saw the coin quiver, flip up onto its edge, and then roll away into the woods.

"And with that, gentlemen, the hunt is on!"

They'd been riding so long that it was now late afternoon, and Kyra was behind the soldiers she'd set to keep watch on the coin. They'd let their mounts graze, and casually notice the coin wiggle and roll away down the path, then they'd nudge their horses forward.

Ned brought his horse up beside Kyra's.

Her life had changed so much in the past day. No longer was she chasing after her best friend. She was *with* the army instead of hiding from them. She was part of the Master Trio of Potioners again.

And she was following a coin as it merrily rolled along through the woods.

"You haven't been on a horse in a while, have you?" Ned asked.

"Do I look that bad? My riding muscles and calluses are completely gone. I feel like an idiot."

"You'll get them back. It'll just take a little bit of time." He gently touched her shoulder. "So tell me about this potion you created—the one that will take down the shape-shifter things."

"The shape-shifter things are called obeekas, and there are at least two with Arlo," Kyra said. "I was hoping you and Hal would be the ones to go after them while I focus on capturing Arlo."

Hal had ridden up on her other side. "Of course we will."

Kyra caught Ned rolling his eyes.

She nudged him with her foot and continued. "It's a concoction using the Cera Truth Serum. Peccant Pentothal is too dangerous to use unless absolutely necessary, and I don't think we need anything that strong anyway. Just something to cast the obeekas in their true form so we can bind them."

"*That* is brilliant," Hal said, his eyes glowing.

"We needed something you two can throw easily, so I created these." She showed them a dozen small balloons she'd filled with the potion. "Just like our old water balloon fights in summer." She felt wistful for a moment thinking about it. Those days were gone forever.

Hal hefted one in his hand. He looked wistful too. "It's a good idea, Kyra. These will work well."

In a town a half day's ride outside Wexford, the coin began moving more erratically, zigging and zagging.

"That strange behavior means the coin is almost home," Kyra said. "We're near Arlo." It had grown dark and was well past dinnertime. Down the street was a large pub blazing with light.

The coin began vibrating as it neared the building.

Kyra slid off her horse and caught the coin in front of the pub. Then everyone dismounted and gathered by the entrance. They all knew their roles.

"There could be innocents inside. Try not to kill anyone." She checked her weapons.

Kyra stepped inside—Hal on the left of her, Ned on the right, the soldiers filing in behind. The pub smelled stale, like grease and old ale.

She spotted Arlo immediately at a gaming table on the far end of the pub, his back to the wall. The position of power. The guy next to him looked weirdly familiar.

"Arlo Abbaduto." Kyra's voice rang out over the sounds of the filled tavern. "You are under arrest by order of the King of Mohr for a plot against the kingdom." The room quieted as everyone turned to look at her. "Do not resist arrest. Anyone who obstructs us will be considered in league with the plot against the kingdom and tried as such."

Silence followed. The eyes on Kyra were unfriendly. Men missing teeth, covered in scars, and clutching mugs of ale leered.

Then Arlo started to laugh. "Ha-ha-ha!"

The crowd joined in. Soon the whole room quaked with laughter.

"So nice of you to come visit, Master Potioners," Arlo said. "I hope you don't mind if we disagree on how this is going to go. You see, you're outnumbered. Men," he shouted, "kill the king's soldiers!"

And suddenly the room broke into motion, the men in the bar surging forward even as the soldiers brandished swords and pulled Kyra and Hal and Ned backward. The air was filled with the clash of metal and shouts and grunts, and fists and boots hitting flesh.

Kyra tried to get a glimpse of Arlo through the melee, but was pushed down to the floor by two brawling men.

Quickly, she stuck them both with Doze needles and shoved them away. Hal and Ned each took a hand and pulled her back on her feet.

There was no way around the tumult. Arlo was right—they were vastly outnumbered. She was going to have to change the odds a bit.

"I'm going to try taking a few people out," Kyra shouted to Hal and Ned as she jumped up on a table.

Needles tipped in Doze rained from the air until Kyra found herself flung up as someone flipped over the table. Her body slammed into the sticky floorboards so hard it jarred every bone in her body.

Kyra gulped in air and scootched across the floor until she found a small clearing where she could stand. Immediately, an elbow caught her in the gut.

She spotted Ned and Hal a few feet in front of her, about three tables away from Arlo, then watched in horror as the concierge's assistant shrank down to a hairy rodent and darted away through the crowd.

"I'll get him!" Hal shouted, running off in the same direction.

The man who'd been sitting on the other side of Arlo grew into a huge troll.

Ned sighed. "Of course I get stuck with the giant one." He moved forward, bashing brawlers out of the way with his baton in one hand, a potion-filled balloon in the other.

Kyra glanced at Arlo. He wasn't even paying attention to her.

He wasn't worried about her at all.

He was enjoying this. The chaos, the fighting, the blood—he was drinking it in. Every now and then he'd clap his hands when a particularly good hit connected.

Kyra stepped close and shouted above the roar of the brawl, "Arlo Abbaduto! Under the name of the King, you are—"

"—enjoying this immensely." Arlo finally turned his attention to her. "It's quite a show you've put on here."

"You aren't going to weasel out of this one, Arlo. We've got you."

"You think you can take me, *Master Potioner*?"

She was out of needles and had already thrown the knife she kept tucked in her waistband at the small of her back.

"Or have you come to join me?" Arlo stood up from his table. "We both know you've turned criminal. That's why you came to me when you needed help finding the princess."

Kyra couldn't help herself. "I came to you because I was desperate. Why did you send me to Ellie the hermit?"

"He made a terrible lackey." Arlo's smile revealed his large mossy teeth. "I thought in your rage at not finding the princess, your little murderer's heart would see fit to take care of him for me."

"I am *not* a murderer."

Arlo began laughing again. "Not a murderer, eh? You tried to kill the princess, you almost killed me once upon a time—there *is* murder in you. You're just like me."

"She wasn't the real princess!" Kyra ducked a mug that smashed on the wall behind her.

"You didn't know that. You were prepared to kill her anyway."

"You're going to prison, Arlo." Kyra resorted to her weapon of last defense: she swung out a fist and landed a solid blow to his jaw.

It hurt her hand.

Arlo swatted her to the floor.

"And arresting me wouldn't be murder?" He leered down at her. "Do you think they're going to slap me on the hands for this and send me on my way? You want me to hang."

Kyra shoved hard on his knee with the ball of her foot and stood as he stumbled. "It would be justice."

"It would be what's in your little murderer's heart." He swatted at her again, but this time she dropped and rolled, taking some of the force out of the blow. Still, it hurt. Fighting him was like fighting a giant boulder with arms.

"Why are you doing this?" she shouted as she came back to her feet again.

"When the Kingdom of Mohr fails, it *will be* the Kingdom of Criminals. *My* kingdom."

Kyra tried to look for an opening.

"And I'll need a queen—one who knows her way around potions, one with royal blood by birth, who can appease our citizens while I take my place. A queen with murder in her heart."

Kyra jumped up on the table directly in front of him, smacking her hands to her thighs.

"What say you, little girl—are you the next Queen of Mohr?"

"I don't think so," she said, and pursed her mouth to blow the poison out of her hands and into his face.

Twenty-eight

Kyra set her potions satchel on the sturdy oak worktable in her old bedroom in the palace. Two days had passed since she'd arrested Arlo, and he was waiting downstairs in the courtroom. She couldn't believe he'd elected to have the serum again. Maybe he thought she'd make another mistake. But there was no way he was getting off this time.

Kyra had decided to make up the dilution in her room. She didn't want to spend one second more in the same room with the criminal than she had to in order to administer the serum.

And she wanted to enjoy this one last time with her potions. As punishment for holding a knife to her mother's throat, Kyra had been forbidden potions work for half a year.

Instead, she was to play the role of a proper lady: wait on the queen, attend royal events, and make herself useful around the castle.

Kyra would rather have poked out her own eyes.

But she knew better than to cross her mother. So she was going to do what she was told. Just this once.

She swirled the last drop of Peccant Pentothal into the dilution and put the cap back on the vial. Sighing, she cleaned up her work space and picked up the truth serum.

In the hall, a maid curtsied as she went by. "Thank you so much for saving the kingdom, my lady."

Kyra hurried past. Everyone in the entire kingdom seemed to think she was some kind of hero now and felt the need to thank her personally. She was used to being somewhat famous—she was the queen's niece and a Master Potioner, but this was a whole new level of fame. It would take some getting used to.

She found Arlo in the same interview cell as the first time they'd met. A scribe sat at one end of the table, and court officials were scattered throughout the room.

Arlo leered when he saw Kyra. "How nice of you to grace us with your presence, *Master Potioner*. Maybe this time you'll succeed in killing me."

"I wouldn't be so cavalier if I were you," Kyra said, setting her bag down on the table, across from him. "You won't be getting out of this."

"We'll see."

Kyra ignored him and carefully squeezed a drop of serum on one of his large manacled hands. He waited—perhaps

for the same reaction as last time—but nothing obvious happened.

Kyra smiled and stood. "I don't need to be here for the interview," she said to the scribe and court officials. "I've seen enough of him to last me a lifetime."

"You've made a mistake," Arlo said as she turned to go. "You think you've got me, girlie, but you don't. Not by a long shot."

He began laughing. The sound filled the chamber, chasing Kyra as she slipped out.

The next day, Kyra heard that this time the serum had worked: Arlo had admitted to everything—plotting against the kingdom, kidnapping the princess and replacing her, manipulating poor soft-in-the-head Ellie the hermit, and everything else to do with the kidnapping.

He did not, however, admit anything about his other crimes. Somehow, his mind was a fierce blank in the kingdom's interrogations. He kept hinting that no one was asking the right questions, and that if only they did, they'd find out everything they wanted to know. Because of what he *might* know, he wouldn't be going near a hangman's noose anytime soon. The king saw him as too valuable a resource to merely execute him.

But if staying alive made Arlo think he'd gotten the best of Kyra, he was totally wrong. She was more than happy to let him rot in the dungeon.

With Arlo behind bars, the queen started planning for a celebration ball in honor of the heroes. She had plenty

of work for Ariana, Fred, and Kyra, and didn't bother to respond when Ariana pointed out that loading them up with work was certainly *not* a reward for heroic services rendered. The queen had just kissed her on the head and sent her off to write out invitations.

Kyra didn't mind the work at all—it was a distraction. Later that day, she went up to Ariana's room and entered without knocking. The doors to the princess's balcony, locked throughout her childhood, stood open. Kyra could hear laughter floating in.

Ariana and Fred. Her gut twisted. She was going to have to get used to this.

Kyra walked out and found her friends lounging on chairs.

Rosie and Langley were cuddled together by the low wall of the parapet. As Rosie ran up, her pink nose in the air, Kyra picked her up and set her on her lap. "Did you lift her, Fred? I think Rosie's gained weight already! You brought her with you to the kitchens, didn't you?"

"Of course. Sofie loves her. She's a lovable creature."

"A lovable creature who's getting pudgy."

"She's not pudgy," Fred said. "She's just jolly. I don't mind her getting fattened up at all." He reached to pat Langley on the head.

"Which you will as well," Ari said, "if you're just going to lounge around here."

"Nothing wrong with lounging." Fred scooted further down in his chair. "We deserve a little nap."

"No time for napping," Kyra said. "Not when there are parties to plan."

"Ugh!" Ariana said. "Don't remind me. I promised Mother I'd do place settings by end of day. What time is it?"

Fred pulled his watch out of his pocket. "Quarter to three." He set it down on the table between them.

"Plenty of time to do that *and* get in a nice ride in. If you two are just going to lie around here, I'm heading out." Ari stood up and brushed her hands off on her pants. "Later, lazybones!"

"Your future wife sure is a sweetheart," Kyra said, though it hurt to joke about the nuptials that were undoubtedly right around the corner.

Fred didn't appear to catch her tone. "I'll say." He settled back with his eyes closed.

Kyra desperately wanted to say something, demand that he explain why he'd kissed her when he was an engaged man; if there'd been anything there between them or if he'd just been messing with her. But she didn't say anything, just watched as he appeared to fall into a deep sleep. She wasn't sure she wanted to know the answer.

She picked up his pocket watch, the one the witch had stolen. And he'd apparently stolen back.

She looked and understood why.

Engraved on the back in tiny writing was PRINCE FREDERICK LANTANA III, OF ARCADIA. He hadn't wanted anyone to find out who he was.

And she'd thought he'd stolen back her necklace to be nice.

The evening of the ball finally arrived, and when it did, Kyra found herself hesitating outside the giant arched doors of the

 269

ballroom. She'd left Rosie in the kitchen with Langley, to be spoiled rotten by Sofie and the staff.

Ariana tramped down the hall, a new green dress swishing around her, and stopped short at the sight of her friend. "You okay?" she asked.

"Yeah," Kyra said. "I just haven't been in there since, you know, I tried to kill you and all."

"I guess you want to relish the moment." Ariana bumped her shoulder playfully.

"Exactly."

"You look like you're going to throw up."

"You can't imagine, Ari, making the decision to kill someone you love. Your whole idea of who you are flips upside down. I went to Arlo for help! I'd become a criminal."

"Kitty." Ariana took her hand. "You know who you are. Nothing can change that. Deep down inside you knew it wasn't really me—that it was really a monster. You're a good person, trust me."

Kyra looked at the doors to the ballroom. That's where it had all happened. She'd stood with a poisoned needle in her hand, and—Arlo had been right—there had been murder in her heart.

"How about"—Ariana put her arm through Kyra's—"we go in together and I'll tell you a secret."

"Really? You've got a secret?" Instead of running away, Kyra leaned in toward her friend and was through the doors and into the ballroom before she knew it.

"I do, but it isn't going public quite yet, so you can't tell anyone about it." Ariana expertly dodged her way through the crowd, ignoring the welcoming hands of people.

Kyra nodded at Ned and Hal as she passed them at the cake table.

Ariana brought Kyra over to an empty spot next to a table stacked with clear crystal goblets. "I'm not marrying Fred."

"What?"

"Mom tried to pretend like the whole thing didn't completely throw her for a loop, but she's really freaked out by the whole fake princess thing. So I took advantage."

"Ari!"

"What? It's the smart thing to do. Anyway, I got her to promise that I could at least pick out my own husband."

"I thought you liked Fred."

"I adore him, but not as a *husband*, Kitty. As a fun and slightly ridiculous friend, or the sometimes annoying brother I never had, but not as a husband."

"Does Fred know?" Kyra took an empty goblet and shakily filled it with amber-colored liquid.

"I told him before dinner."

"Is he, um, unhappy?"

Ariana looked right into Kyra's olive-colored eyes, her own eyes sparkling. "Why do you ask?"

When Kyra didn't answer, Ariana whisked the goblet out of Kyra's hand and said, "Why don't you go ask him? He's right across the room."

Kyra looked, but Fred was turned away from her.

Ariana went on. "Is he talking to Hal? How did Fred even get in there with all of those women mobbing the guy?" She left Kyra standing there, gobletless, and half in shock.

Before Kyra could even begin to think seriously about talking to Fred, the Duchess Genria was at her side. "So, you've had quite the adventure."

"Hello, Mother," Kyra responded, resigned.

"I hope you're taking your punishment seriously. I've recovered from your bad manners at the ducal palace, but your poor father is still in shock. That little show you put on in the dining hall probably took years off his life."

"I had to, Mom," Kyra said. "I was saving the kingdom." She didn't mention that her father was doing just fine, because it was impossible to argue with the duchess. Her father had even made the trip here to attend the ball, and was, in fact, across the room right now laughing at something the king was saying.

"Yes, well, you could have tried something a little less exciting around your father. You know how excitement upsets his digestion."

"I'll try to remember that next time."

"Yes, you do that." The duchess half lowered her lids. "I spoke with my friend Muriel, the witch who you had the little altercation with. She said it was all a misunderstanding."

Kyra's breath caught. "She tried to *eat* me."

"She was just trying to scare you." The duchess's green eyes swept over Kyra. "If you would get some training, you would never be at the mercy of another witch."

"I did just fine with potions."

"But you could do so much more if you could harness both magic *and* potions. Please consider training, Kyra. I'd feel better knowing you were safe out there in the world if you had *all* of your gifts at your disposal."

People were dancing now, in a swirl of colored dresses and shining faces. Kyra watched them flit by. Arlo had known an awful lot about how the castle operated to be able to pull off what he had. Were there people in this room right now who'd assisted him? One of those shining faces could be a traitor and Kyra wouldn't even know it. She couldn't douse the whole room in truth serum.

What if she could use her Sight to find out?

The duchess patiently sipped her mead, watching the dancers.

"I'll think about it," Kyra said.

If the duchess was surprised, she did a good job of hiding it. "We'll need to find you a teacher. Muriel really is a skilled witch—"

"Mom!"

"—but you seem to harbor some ill feelings toward her. I'm not quite sure I trust her if it comes to that, but apprentice/teacher contracts have a nonharm spell on them usually. She doesn't have the Sight, though. It's a rare gift. I'll have to do some looking into this. . . ."

As the duchess began moving away, Kyra shouted, "I just said I'd *think* about it."

The duchess kept going, not bothering to respond.

Kyra had no idea what she'd just gotten herself into. She picked up an empty goblet and began filling it with mead.

An extremely handsome young man approached her, in full royal gear complete with a velvet coat, and Kyra almost dropped her glass when she realized it was Fred.

Fred took the goblet from her. "How sweet, you got me a glass." He took a sip of the mead. "This is good! Gotta love those bee-keeping monks."

Kyra caught a glimpse of Ariana across the hall.

It was all well and good for Ariana to think that she and Fred were just friends, but how could Fred not be in love with Ariana?

"Ariana told me she canceled the wedding," Kyra blurted out before she could stop herself.

"She did."

"I'm sorry. I can't imagine you're happy about that."

"Why would you think that?"

"Well, she's Ariana. How can you not love her?"

Fred's mouth lifted on one side. "That's true. It *is* difficult not to love her."

"And you won't get half a kingdom anymore, either."

"Maybe I could woo her." Fred rubbed the stem of his glass. "I'm sure she'd have me if it was by her own choice."

Kyra's stomach dropped. "What?"

"Kyra." Fred caught Kyra's eyes. "I'm not in love with Ariana and I don't want half the kingdom."

"You don't?"

He shook his head. "But I might stick around for a little while longer. There are some interesting things in the Kingdom of Mohr."

"Like what?"

"Like a certain funny and extremely talented potioner."

Kyra took a breath. "I have to warn you, Hal isn't that great as a boyfriend. He's pretty self-absorbed."

The edges of Fred's mouth turned up a fraction more. "Kyra, I think you know who I mean."

"Is this because you found out I'm a princess?"

He shot her a look.

Kyra smiled inwardly, but she didn't quite know what to say.

She didn't have to say anything, because Fred continued. "May I ask you one thing?"

"Mm-hm."

"What in the world were you doing wearing that ridiculous underwear when I first met you?" He started laughing.

"You try picking out reasonable underwear when you're fleeing an entire staff of palace guards!"

"Wouldn't it have made sense to pack *before* you attempted to kill the princess?"

Kyra looked at him seriously. "I wasn't planning to run away after I killed the princess. I wouldn't have been able to live with myself after having murdered my cousin and my best friend. I was planning a nice trip to prison, and from there to the executioner's. So when my dart didn't kill the princess, all I could think was, I've got to get out of here so I can finish the job later. After I finally ditched the guards, I had to hide in a dumbwaiter for a good four hours before I could sneak into my room and away."

Fred had been listening intently, but started laughing again. "You hid in the dumbwaiter?"

"Yes."

"What if they'd called it down to send up some tea or something?"

"They would have been in for a surprise."

"I'm glad you escaped, Kyra," Fred said, looking serious again. "And that I found you."

"Me too," Kyra said, glancing up at him. "It wouldn't have been much of a life trying to live in the dumbwaiter."

Fred leaned down and kissed Kyra full on the lips.

Kyra pulled away. "How do you know I'm interested in you? Just because you've decided I'm worth hanging around for doesn't mean I feel the same way."

Fred cocked his head at her. *"Really?"*

"Oh, okay," Kyra said.

Then she kissed him back.

Acknowledgments

THE SIGN OF A LIFE WELL LIVED is that there are always too many people to thank.

A few of those who helped bring *Poison* to print: Bridget's writing family—the Madison, Wisconsin, Writers' Group: Georgia Beaverson, Judy Bryan, Emily Kokie, Michael Kress-Russick, Rosanne Lindsay, Julie Shaull, Kashmira Sheth, and Melinda Starkweather.

Friends and fellow authors who lent their insights: April Henry, Janet Piehl, and Emily Whitman.

Publishing pros and industry shepherds: Michael Stearns (agent and friend), Tamson Weston (who bought it), Catherine Onder and Hayley Wagreich (who saw it through), and Stephanie Lurie and the rest of the dream team at Disney-Hyperion.

And always and ever, those who loved it first and fiercest: Richard Zinn (Daddo)—"Okay, *now* you can read it"—and Barrett Dowell, husband, best friend, and soul mate.

"Thanks for everything. Love to you all."